Racing California

Racing California

Janet Nichols Lynch

Holiday House / New York

Library of Congress Cataloging-in-Publication Data
Lynch, Janet Nichols, 1952–
Racing California / Janet Nichols Lynch. — 1st ed.
p. cm.
Summary: High school senior Evan is conflicted when he is recruited for
the prestigious Amgen Tour of California bicycle race by one of his heroes,
and must decide whether to pursue his love of racing or go to college after
he graduates from his Arizona high school.
ISBN 978-0-8234-2363-7 (hardcover)
[1. Bicycle racing—Fiction. 2. Competition (Psychology)—Fiction.
3. Teamwork (Sports)—Fiction. 4. California—Fiction.] I. Title.
PZ7.L9847Rac 2012
[Fic]—dc23
2011025952

Author's Note

Any information in this novel pertaining to real people, living and dead, is accurate. The Amgen Tour of California is a real race, but the account of its running within these pages is a work of fiction. Names, characters, and incidents are the product of the author's imagination.

Acknowledgments

In viewing the Amgen Tour of California and cycling most of the course, I had lots of support, including Tim, Caitlin, and Sean Lynch; Joyce Fanshier; Mark and Bridget Fischer; Nina Lynch; Marsha and Roy Rocklin; and Caryl and Terry Schonig. I am grateful to my lifelong cycling pal Penney Olson, who guided me on a tour of Phoenix cycling spots and, as my first reader, gave me helpful suggestions. Thanks also to Doug Olson for lending me the names of his companies for Evan's team. Carl Fischer helped me with the Spanish and Penney with the French. Breaking Away Bicycle Tours showed me how a great touring company is run, and my "home teams" Visalia Triathlon Club, Visalia Runners, and Southern Sierra Cyclists keep me energized.

To Penney

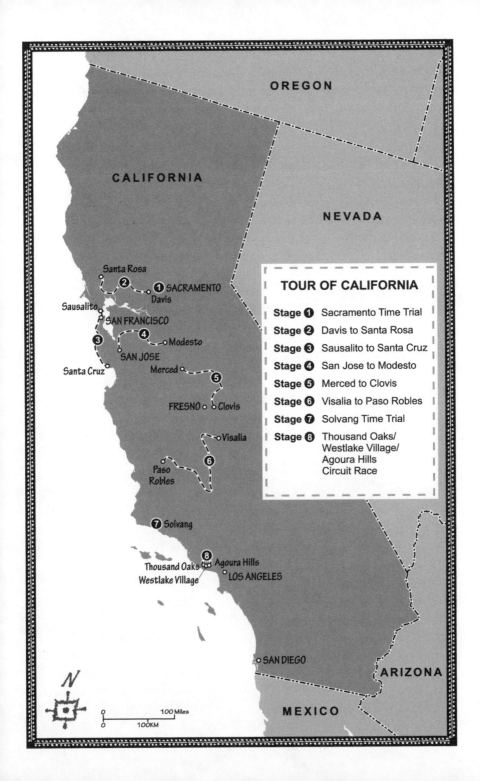

Part One

Training Camp

Chapter One

Ouch! I rise out of the saddle to stomp on the pedals and my quads scream in pain. We're slogging up the steep grade toward Saguaro Lake against a wicked headwind, in the brisk December sunshine. The seventy or so pro cyclists grunt and mutter expletives in various languages: English, French, Italian, Kazakh, Spanish, and Dutch. Lots of famous teams—Garmin-Cervélo, BISSELL, SpiderTech, and Jelly Belly—are represented at this winter training camp here in Phoenix.

"*¡Ay carajo! ¡Me estoy muriendo!*"

I grin. It's not one of the Spaniards telling me he's dying, but my buddy Jay Stevens. Since we're studying for our AP Spanish final, we made a bet to speak only Spanish during winter break, and the one who says the first English word loses. We work for Arizona Cycling Tours, the company that is staging this training camp. We're supposed to help guide the pros along the Salt River into plateau country, but I hardly think anyone will get lost with the entourage of motorcycles and cars carrying team managers, trainers, *directeurs sportifs*, mechanics, *soigneurs*, medics, extra wheels, and bicycles.

I'm amazed we haven't been dropped, but I know it's a matter of fitness. Some of the Europeans are jet-lagged, and many of the riders have laid off the bike since the end of racing season in September. They're here to get in form for the Amgen Tour of California in February, nearly a month before the pro cycling season gets under way in Europe with Paris-Nice.

Jay's tongue is hanging nearly to the asphalt. Gasping between words, he whispers, "Dashiell . . . Shipley . . . *está aquí.*"

I get spiky tingles on my arms. Dashiell Shipley—Tour de France winner, reigning U.S. Pro Road Champion, my idol. But Jay has already pointed out cycling stars George Hincapie, Chris Horner, and Dave Zabriskie, and he's been wrong every time. I look all around me but don't spot the red-and-gold jersey of Dash's team, Kronen. Although Dash is American, he rides for a team sponsored by a Dutch beer. All the pro teams are composed of mixed nationalities.

One more shuddering gasp is the last I hear of Jay. Beneath my armpit I watch him slip through the peloton and off the back. I move up, positioning myself behind the lead rider, who's battling the wind. He's wearing a generic blue jersey and plain black shorts rather than a team kit. I've got on a green *Equipo Rana Verde* jersey, which I got for 50 percent off on eBay when that team went belly-up.

The lead rider surges forward, not like he's going to take a flyer, but he just gradually applies more pressure on the pedals. I hang on to his wheel. He slows; I slow. He surges again, pressing a fierce pace; I go with him. After his third push the rider sits up, shifts around, and glares at me. He's got sharp cheekbones, square white teeth, and bronze hair dangling beneath his helmet. It's a chilling moment. I'm staring straight into the face of Dashiell Shipley. He's slightly breathless from bucking the wind, while I'm cozily tucked in the shelter of his slipstream. Cyclists draft like race cars, and the guy in back is only doing about 60 percent of the work.

"Well, go on!" Dash yells at me, punching the air with a straight arm. "¡Más rápido!"

It's pure adrenaline that snaps my legs into action. I whip around him, bound out of the saddle, and sprint like I'm going for King of the Mountain points. At this searing pace I could bonk, but what keeps me alive is knowing what Dash doesn't: the summit is less than a half mile away. I hope I can hang on till then. If I don't have the legs, I've got the will. Whoa, am I tripping or what? I'm riding with Dash Shipley! Dash is, like, chasing *me*!

He catches me easily, within two hundred yards. He bounds around me, but I stick to his wheel like Krazy Glue. I won't let him go, I won't, even though my lungs are gonna explode. Focus, determination. Pain is my friend. I keep my eyes peeled on his rear wheel, a scant three inches ahead of my front one. Meanwhile, a dozen other riders attack and catch us. The breakaway is tight and intense. I've got no breathing room, and I feel the heat of packed, sweating bodies. I'm trapped, wedged in with some of the best cyclists in the world. Hell, what have I gotten myself into? Do I really know what I'm doing? Handlebars gouge into my hip, causing me to turn my head.

Slam. I'm flat on the asphalt, my cheek, shoulder, and left leg on fire. Bodies and bicycles thud over me and around me like heavy duffle bags. There's cursing and scraping metal. Me, the hired help, stacked it! I lie at the bottom of the pile, waiting my turn to get up. The peloton catches us. Riders weave through the fallen guys, sometimes over body parts— *ouch!*—such as my fingers. Team motorcycles and cars pull up along the roadside to assist their riders. One rider twists his handlebars back into place. Another guy stands and waits, blood streaming from his elbow as his mechanic makes a wheel change. Someone else is yanking on a stuck chain.

I'm having difficulty getting up, my right foot twisted in an awkward position, so that I can't kick out my heel to disengage from the pedal. None of the riders are hurt badly enough to abandon; at least no one sailed into the cactus. One by one the riders mount their bikes and roll out of sight, the entourage of support vehicles following them. I'm still sprawled on the pavement.

Jay catches up and jumps off his bike. *"¡Qué lástima!"*

He unfastens the Velcro on my right shoe, so I slide my foot out. I slowly stand and pat myself, inspecting the damage. No broken bones. The shoulder of my cool new *Equipo Rana Verde* jersey is ripped, and the expensive tights my mom splurged on for Christmas are shredded knee to ankle.

"¿Qué pasó?" Jay asks.

"I touched a wheel," I reply in English, in no mood for our little Spanish game, which now sounds stupid.

"Whoa, Evan! You really beefed it! You okay?" asks Jay, also resorting to English, without mentioning he won the bet.

I twist my face away from him. The throbbing burn of road rash hurts less than my pride. Abrasions from bike crashes are not usually deep, just a fine layer of skin scraped off that stings like hell, leaving a wound that weeps blood and water through tiny pinpoints of raw flesh.

"Hey, man, it happens to the best. Remember when Levi Leipheimer touched wheels with Lance Armstrong in the two thousand nine Tour of California?"

"Yeah." Together, Jay and I have pored over that video and numerous other racing clips posted on YouTube.

"He ate asphalt and went on to win the TOC for the third time in a row!"

"Just call me Levi." We have a shaky laugh, and then I add, "Dude, know who's wheel I touched? Dash's!"

"Told ya he was here, bro. Looks like you found him the hard way."

"I was right out in front, man. With Dash Shipley!"

"He must've laid off the bike a long time."

"I know, I know. But still." I try to brush some of the gravel out of my leg wounds, but it doesn't help. I'll have to get fixed up at the lunch break, when we return to the hotel in Tempe. Like all serious riders, I shave my legs, so the cleanup won't be bad. Standing in the road on the ball of my stocking foot, I bend over to wrench my shoe out of the pedal.

It's then I notice a plain black Mercedes, no team name or sponsor logos plastered over it, parked on the side of the road. A man in the driver's seat with a closely cropped gray beard is talking on a BlackBerry, and another guy with a slick black ponytail and Euro shades is in the backseat writing on a clipboard. The driver is staring right at us.

"Who are they?" I mutter.

"We could go over and find out."

"No. What if that one guy is talking to Ben, complaining that an employee is riding recklessly, causing crashes?"

"Hmm. We better roll."

I wiggle my fingers—sore, but not broken—and slip on my shoe. I pick up my bike, spin both wheels, check the brakes and the gears. Everything seems okay, and we're back on the road.

When the sleek black car passes us, neither man looks our way.

Our boss, Ben Rayno, owner and manager of Arizona Cycling Tours, has rented his staff a room at the hotel, even though we're all local and return to our homes at night. In the bathroom I carefully peel my clothing away from the dried blood. Ouch! Sucking air between clenched teeth, I slowly ease into a warm tub to scour my scrapes. After patting myself dry and applying Neosporin, I pull on the same grody cycling clothes I wore in the morning. I didn't think to bring a change of clothes, but then no one ever plans on stacking it.

Jay is waiting for me, seated on the corner of one of the beds, poring over the recent issue of *VeloNews*. I feel better cleaned up, but stiffness is bound to set in later.

We go downstairs to the banquet room Ben has reserved for the camp guests. There's no waiting for the buffet of chicken breasts and pasta, and we load our plates high. Ben warned us not to stalk the pros, so we retreat to an unoccupied table in the corner. Food only tastes this great after sixty or so miles of hard riding. Jay and I slip easily into Spanish as we plan how we will take on our afternoon chores. With the buzz of all the foreign languages in the room, we fit right in.

A busboy comes by to clear our plates. He hands me a note with no name on it. I open it, thinking it's instructions from Ben, wondering why he didn't just text me or Jay.

The message is written in Spanish. "*Visítenos en el cuarto 315.*"

I lean across the table toward Jay, holding up the note so

he can read it. "Got any idea who's staying in room three fifteen?" I ask in English.

"Nope."

"You think it's about the crash? Someone wants to beat the shit out of me for knocking him down?"

"Naw. If you ride, you go down. It's inevitable."

"What's it about then?"

He shrugs. "Glory's dad hired a hit man?"

Jay knows the Albrights aren't crazy about lowly me dating their golden girl. "That's not even funny, bro."

"Who's laughing?" Jay has beady eyes, a black unibrow, and a long, horsey face. He's funniest when he's trying to look serious.

I stare at the note. Finally, I heave a sigh and push back my chair. "Guess I'll go see."

"Wait. Give me the note. If no one ever sees you again, I can hand this over to the cops."

I shoot him a disgusted look. Jay has seen way too much TV, but then maybe I haven't seen enough. I tap the note on the table a few times, then drop it into his palm.

As I'm taking the elevator up to the third floor my pulse speeds. Am I in trouble? Why was the note in Spanish? Whoever they are, they better hurry it up. We're supposed to be back on our bikes in less than an hour.

When I knock on the door of room 315, it is opened by Gray Beard of the Mercedes.

"*¡Hola!*" He ushers me into to the deluxe suite with a handshake. "*¿Habla inglés?*"

"*Sí.* I mean, yes."

"*Bueno.* Good. That makes it easier. I'm Mike Townsend, manager of this outfit." He leads me to Black Ponytail. "This is Rainier Laurent, our *directeur sportif.*"

Anyone who follows pro cycling knows the name. He's the

directeur sportif who masterminded Dashiell Shipley's Tour de France win. If he's here, then Dash is certain to be. What in the hell is going on?

Townsend waves his hand around. "You probably know some of our guys."

Settled deeply into an armchair, his hands clasped behind his head, Dash smiles at me just the way he smiles into the TV camera when Bob Roll interviews him on NBC. He wears his hair longish, swept across his forehead. He's known in cycling as a really nice guy, even though drug-use allegations clouded his Tour de France victory. Now I see why he wasn't wearing the Kronen jersey: he's switching teams.

"You were tearing up that mountain this morning," he says to me.

"For a little while."

"But then you are known as a climber."

"And *Equipo Rana Verde* is kaput," says Mike Townsend. "I suppose you're looking for a new team."

I realize my mouth is hanging open, and I'm blinking rapidly. "Uh . . . I think—"

"Have you signed a new contract yet?" blurts Townsend.

"This is kinda funny. You've got me mixed up with—"

"You *are* Alejandro Mendez, aren't you?" Townsend asks, his eyebrows shooting up.

I have to laugh. It's easy to see why they've mistaken my identity. I'm short and slight like the flyweight Spanish climbing specialist. I've got some Hopi Indian on my dad's side and Italian on my mom's. I've been speaking Spanish with Jay all day and wearing a Spanish team's jersey. "Uh . . . no," I finally answer. "I'm Evan Boroughs. I work for Ben Rayno, the guy who's putting this camp on."

A loud guffaw erupts from the far sofa. I see an unkempt head of woolly brown hair. "This is rich!" says Bernard Nagle.

Obviously if Dash and Rainier Laurent defected from Kronen, Dash's well-known lieutenant would follow. Looking around, I also recognize two other riders, Dutch brothers Joris and Dedrick Pieters, who were domestiques on the Kronen team. Domestiques are the workhorses in cycling, who exhaust themselves hauling around food and drink, bucking the wind, and pulling along the lead riders so that they can spare their energy for the win.

"You do race, don't ya?" Dash asks me. "How's your technical riding?"

"Just okay," I reply honestly. "I take it easy on the descents and don't enter the crits."

"I like to avoid the criteriums myself," says Dash. They're fast, vicious races held on short, circular courses, in which half the field sometimes goes down in a bloody heap. "What are your biggest wins?"

"Mostly hill climbs. Mount Lemmon, Durango, Los Alamos. I'm still in high school and—"

"Ah! You are just a boy," exclaims Rainier Laurent, shaking his head. He speaks perfect English, but with a French accent.

The ends of Bernard's mouth slide up to enclose his bulbous schnoz. "I love it! This just gets better!"

Dash holds up his palm. "Hold it. Henri Cornet won the Tour de France at the age of nineteen."

"*Oui,* in 1904," says Rainier with a chuckle.

"At twenty, Peter Sagan won two stages of Paris-Nice *and* two stages of the Tour of California," argues Dash.

"This . . ." Pointing at me, Bernard laughs harder. "This is not Peter Sagan."

I feel my face burn, the road rash on my cheek stinging. Bernard is known as a "colorful character." Before a TV camera he often makes off-the-cuff, inappropriate comments, which he has to retract later. I shouldn't take him personally, but already I don't like the guy.

"What did you place in the U.S. Amateur Nationals?" Townsend asks.

I shrug. "I've never entered. I mostly study and work."

"Where'd you get the legs?" asks Dash.

"Arizona Cycling Tours offers trips all over the western states. This past summer riding was a big part of my job, but it was just, you know, guiding tours."

Dash grins. "You're a very talented rider."

"Wow, thanks." How is anyone—especially Jay—going to believe Dash told me this?

Dash sits up in his chair, rubbing his chin. "I could use a guy like you to lead me up a couple of climbs in the Tour of California."

"But one who is not so young," says Rainier.

"And we've got Salvatore Netti," interjects Bernard.

"You've got Sal?" I exclaim. The Italian climber often wins King of the Mountains in European stage races.

"We're working on it," says Townsend.

"*And* you've got me," Bernard says to the ceiling. He sits up, facing Dash. "*And* you're favored to win."

"Favored," says Dash. "But you know Temir Laptev won last year, and he's returning to reclaim his title. I'll also have to contend with Fernando Iglesias, the Vuelta a España champ, and there's . . . Klaus." At the mention of Klaus Grunwald the room gets real quiet.

"And that other guy," Bernard says finally.

"Right," says Dash, grinning. "The one we haven't even thought of."

Townsend peers into his BlackBerry. Dash rises from his chair to hook the straps of his bib shorts over his shoulders. I'm slow to realize they're done with me.

I make a show of checking my watch. "Gotta get things set up for this afternoon. It's great to meet you," I say to Dash. "I'll be rooting for you in the Tour of California. What's the name of your new team?"

"We haven't settled on a sponsor yet," blurts Townsend. "We've a number of good prospects though, even some here in Phoenix."

"Good luck with that."

"We won't need luck," Townsend says pointedly. "We've got Dash Shipley."

"Of course," I say, backing out of the room.

No sponsor, no team. Everyone knows that. So I almost got offered a contract on a pro cycling team. If there were actually a team. If I were actually someone else.

Chapter Two

I always try to get in a few extra miles any way I can. Riding into Tempe this morning seemed like a much better idea then than it does now when I'm wiped out. It's dark and rush hour, but I've got flashing micro lights, and I'm used to commuting in traffic. I shift down to a low gear to spin out the lactic acid in my muscles.

I've got lots to mull over. Anyone who watched the Tour de France last summer knows Dash Shipley got shafted by his own team, Kronen. It's true that all riders on a team must work together to help their leader win, but it's possible for this loyalty to shift if another teammate gets the advantage. Climbing up the

Col d'Izoard, a desolate scorcher in the Alps, Dash was pedaling smooth, while Klaus Grunwald halted at the base of each turn of the crank, pedaling squares. The Kronen team manager demanded that Dash wait for the German, telling him he was only three minutes behind, when it was more like six. As the Tour progressed, Klaus faded as Dash got stronger. By the beginning of the third week, Klaus abandoned with gastroenteritis, while Dash went on to victory. Even then, Kronen played down their new Tour champion and stated to the media that ailing Klaus Grunwald would be back with a vengeance next year.

It's a scenario that has been repeated several times in Tour history. When one team has two big stars like Bernard Hinault and Greg LeMond on the French team *La Vie Claire* in the 1980s or Alberto Contador and Lance Armstrong on Astana in 2009, there's bitterness and an eventual split. Dash was justified in leaving Kronen, but it seems he didn't look before he leaped. He's really popular with American cycling fans, but I guess not corporate America. It's damned expensive to sponsor a team. I hope Mike Townsend can find Dash and his team backing by the Tour of California.

Today was totally bomb, even if I did crash. Dash was impressed with my climbing. I gotta be happy about that. I wish I could go all out in racing, but it means riding two hundred or more miles per week; but just as the season gets under way in the spring, I've got AP exams and finals to study for, and every summer I've worked, saving for college.

My mom once told me, "You'll never make any money riding that bike," but last summer I proved her wrong. Some weeks I made more money in tips than salary. Arizona Cycling has excursions in great spots like the Canadian Rockies, the Sierra Nevada, and the Utah Canyonlands. Every week was a new tour and every day was an amazing biking adventure.

Ben drove one support and gear van, while Jay and I were supposed to take turns driving the second SAG wagon and cycling with the guests. Early in the summer Jay, who's an awesome techie and plans to major in mechanical engineering, decided he'd rather drive, repair bicycles, and photograph the guests, while I preferred to ride.

Each day on tour at about four o'clock, Ben was eager to sweep the course, scoop up the stragglers into his van, and head for the hotel in time to shower before cocktail hour. I always told him to go on ahead; I'd see the guests in. I didn't mind a bit, riding with the businessman from Ohio who signed up in December thinking he could lose that extra thirty pounds by June, then riding farther back to chat with the elderly couple from Holland, or riding even farther back to check on the two hilarious young women from Toronto who somehow thought spin class would prepare them to ride seventy-five- to one-hundred-mile days on the road.

After riding 6,558 miles in three months, I returned to Phoenix to start my senior year. Sitting at a desk just felt wrong. The teacher's voice would fade, and although I was staring straight at what was projected on the screen, I would see the Grand Tetons. Since then, I've tried to keep the long distance cycling up, doing one 100-miler per weekend, but I haven't always found the time. When Ben asked me if I wanted to work this pro cycling training camp over winter break, I jumped at the chance. And today I met Dash Shipley! I rode with him. How awesome is that?

When I turn onto my street, I'm surprised to see Glory's black pearl Acura TL parked in our driveway. She and I are fairly new, only a couple of months. We go to different schools and don't see much of each other, but we're planning to attend the University of Arizona in Tucson together next year.

Glory wouldn't just drop by without my being home, which

means she's here to visit my sister, the enemy. Meredith is two years older and a sophomore at the University of California in Santa Barbara. She wishes I were never born, but when she came home for winter break last week, she and Glory hit it off. Meredith wants to be a doctor, the same as Glory and me, which makes me think that's too many doctors. Not all of us are going to make it.

I step into the warm yellow kitchen, and everyone is gathered around the table having munchies and drinks.

"Evan, your cheek!" Glory touches her hand to her own soft face as if she can feel my pain. She looks into my eyes, and I look into hers. I want to lean over and kiss her, but I'm too grody to go near her.

Meredith sniffs the air as if something rotten just entered the room.

"Aw, no, Ren!" Mom exclaims. "I knew something like this would happen." She stoops down to inspect my scrapes peeking through my shredded tights. "You need to clean out those abrasions right away."

"I already did."

She pokes her fingers into the tears of the cloth as if she doesn't believe me.

"How'd the first day of camp go?" Dad asks excitedly.

"Isn't it obvious?" asks Mom.

Dad waves his fingers at my legs indicating that my injuries are superficial. He used to race in college, but when Meredith and I were little, Mom guilt-tripped him into taking a long hiatus from the bike. He's only just gotten back into it. My boss, Ben, is one of his cycling buddies, which is how I got my job. "Did you get to meet any of the pros?" asks Dad.

Mom lays her palm against her chest as the center of her body caves. Lately she's been having these sudden attacks.

I touch her shoulder. "You okay, Mom?"

Her "yeah" comes out more like a groan. Her hand sweeps down her body to press into her right side.

"It's an ulcer, I bet," says Dad. "You work too damn hard, Connie."

"Stress doesn't help." Meredith glares at me with her dark, judging eyes.

Mom's hands move to her upper back as Glory watches. "Maybe it's your gallbladder," she suggests.

Mom gives Glory a sharp shake of her head. It's not exactly rude, but it's pretty cold.

"That old fart Wilkens doesn't know squat, Mom," says Meredith. "You should go to a doctor who can figure out what's wrong with you."

Mom straightens, her face smooth again. Like other times, the sharp pains have subsided as quickly as they attacked. "Dr. Wilkens has already referred me to a gastroenterologist at the hospital. I'll be seeing him in a few weeks."

Mom and Dad both work at St. Joseph's Hospital in Phoenix, Mom running the intensive care unit and Dad helping to deliver babies, what he calls playing catch. Mom is one tough cookie. She sometimes drops her head and taps her skull, remarking, "See the scars?" She's referring to her breaking through "the glass ceiling," which kept women from advancing in hospital administration.

I shower and change, and then we eat. All winter break Meredith has been crabbing about my music, Dad's clothes, and the way Mom keeps house, but now she acts all bubbly, chatting with Glory about medical internships. Mom and Dad offer suggestions about applications. I'm too beat to try to get a word in, so I just scarf down Dad's awesome tri-tip.

Finally he asks about bike camp again, and I get to tell my story about meeting Dash Shipley and being mistaken for a Spanish pro.

"Amazing, Ren!" Dad's smile grows nearly too big for his face. He doesn't have much mobility in his neck, but rather than turn his whole body in my direction, he peers out of the corner of his eye at me. "You must've been climbing well!"

"It was just that little hill going into Saguaro Lake, nothing like the Tour of California. Can you imagine racing eight days, seven hundred miles?"

"Sounds like a sore butt to me," says Meredith. "What schools have you applied to, Glory?"

"UCLA, Berkeley, Harvard." Glory's glittering eyes smile into mine. "I've pretty much settled on UA, though."

"That's stupid!" whoops Meredith. "Why pick dumpy Arizona? If you were truly committed, you'd go to a more prestigious university."

"Evan is going to UA, and he's committed." Under the table, Glory grips my quad. "Aren't you?"

"Uh . . . sure," I say.

Meredith sneers. "That's real commitment."

In my mind I hide my goat. When Meredith and I fought as little kids, my parents would often side with her, saying, "She's older," or "She's a girl," which seemed like lame excuses for letting her get her way. "Don't let her get your goat," my dad would say. I had a little plastic farm set, which I hardly played with. I dug it out of my closet, took out the goat, and hid it in my sock drawer. I point my fork in Meredith's direction. "Look, when the guys take off for spring racing in Colorado or California, I'm left behind, studying away."

"You were on your bike the whole summer," she says.

"I was getting paid! Nearly every dollar I earned went into my college fund. All you have to show for yourself is students loans, so don't tell me I'm not committed."

Glory's hand falls away; her eyes widen. I realize my voice is raised, and in her family no one ever speaks above a low, even tone. Yea for Meredith! She got my goat. She succeeded in making me look bad in front of Glory.

After dinner Glory and I settle on the sofa, alone in the rec room with some of our favorite tunes pumping out of my iPod through the speakers. I bump my sore leg against the coffee table and groan.

"Oh! Are you okay?" Glory tilts her head in a cute, concerned way.

"Just a little stiff."

"Maybe Ben won't make you ride tomorrow."

"I want to ride." Glory doesn't understand what a big deal it was for me to ride with Dash Shipley, so there's no point in even talking about it. I change the subject to the snowboarding trip we're planning to take with her parents to their cabin in Colorado over the Martin Luther King, Jr. holiday. I'm more excited about being asked along than the actual snowboarding. So far her parents have been rather cool toward me, and being invited on this trip is a major breakthrough. I start listing the stuff we need to bring when I notice Glory isn't paying attention. "Glory?"

"Huh? Oh, sorry. What's that?"

"I said we should remember to pack—"

"Meredith can really be blunt sometimes," she blurts. "What if she's right? What if I am being stupid for attending UA?"

"You still have time to think about it," I suggest. "You can hold off your final decision until you see where you're accepted."

"Don't you want us to be together at UA?"

I stroke her long, silky hair. "Of course I do, babe. But I want what's right for you."

Glory runs her crystal pendant up and down its silver chain.

"Dad's not so well, and Mom still gets depressed. If I went back East, I'm afraid that . . . Oh, I don't know." She snuggles against my chest.

Who knows what will happen to us next fall? I don't want to think about it, not now when I've got Glory at my side, soft and warm. I kiss the top of her head and lift her onto my lap.

She puts her arms around me and presses her fingers into my nape. I close me eyes and say, "Ah."

"Where did you get the nickname Ren?"

"It's dumb. Only my family uses it."

"But why?"

"You know in the Renaissance, men were expected to be good at everything—science, poetry, music, fencing. Well, my parents called me Renaissance Boy because I was interested in a bunch of stuff: karate, drums, soccer, computers."

"It still fits you. Can I call you Ren?"

"Please don't. I love it when you say my name in your sexy voice."

"Evan," she whispers, her breath warm on my ear. We kiss. It hurts my face.

After I walk Glory out to her car, I trudge upstairs to my room. I've got a poster of Dash Shipley wearing the Tour de France winner's yellow jersey with DASH TO DONATE written in red across the bottom.

The year before last, Dash took a season off to donate a kidney to his six-year-old son, Logan. When interviewed about it, he said, "It's human instinct to protect our young. Any father would do what I did to save his child's life." I believe this is true. I know my parents would do the same for Meredith and me, and yet Dash racing with only one kidney seems heroic. The less he made of it, the more the media broadcasted it. He organized his foundation Dash to Donate to increase organ donor designations on drivers' licenses and enrollment in the bone marrow registry. All of this makes him one of the most popular American pros, but when he tried to return to racing last year, no one believed he could make a comeback. He had a hard time finding a team until Kronen picked him up. Now, it seems, he's out of work again.

I resist the urge to fall into bed and get out my foam roller. It's an eighteen-inch cylinder that I use daily as a sort of poor man's massage. I need to roll out the spent tissue in my muscles to get the blood flowing, then stretch so I won't be stiff when I get up tomorrow. I start pushing the roller up and down my calves, quads, and glutes. I'm working my way up my back when I jump up with a sudden urge to Google Alejandro Mendez.

I find out he has more King of the Mountains titles than actual wins. I don't actually look anything like him in the face, but our physiques are almost the same. I also look up Mike Townsend and find out he is a San Diego businessman in his midforties who sold his sporting events staging company to become first a race director and now a team manager. In a *Bloomberg Businessweek* article he is pictured with "longtime friend" Dashiell Shipley.

After I finish rolling and stretching, I lie in bed wide awake. Crap, I need sleep, but my thoughts are running a mile a minute. I loved what went on today—the tight, fast peloton; the entourage of support vehicles; the sleek, high-tech bicycles that the Euro TV commentators call machines. I want to be a part of pro cycling, but how? Maybe I can be a team doctor. Or if I don't make MD, I can be a physical therapist. Who am I kidding? I want to be a rider.

I begin humming softly, "Hark, the Herald Angels Sing."

I sing in the men's chorus at school, and what's so cool about Christmas songs is there are so many of them that have *glory* or *Gloria* in them. I imagine her intense blue eyes and her cheeks, pink with the cold, against the snow and pines of Aspen. Finally I drift from daydreams to real dreams of my girl, Gloria Elizabeth Albright.

Chapter Three

I wasn't looking the day I found Glory. I was on my bike darting through Scottsdale traffic, and up ahead was this skirt, a preppy uniform skirt, kind of short and swinging so sweet. I love skirts and any girls' clothes that leave something to the imagination. My imagination must've been running wild because the next thing I knew I was about to run a red light, cars already entering the intersection. I yanked the bike hard right. My front wheel hit the curb, I went flying over the bars and landed sprawled on my back.

Now I was in front of the skirt. It descended at my side, and long tendrils of honey-brown hair tickled my face.

"Oh my god! Don't move!"

I wasn't going anywhere. She smelled yummy, flowery and fruity. Small, firm fingers pressed tentatively at the base of my skull and fondled each vertebra of my neck. "Are you a nurse?"

"Doctor. Want to be."

"Me, too! Ow!"

"Hold still! Wiggle your toes!"

"At the same time?"

Her giggle was ripply. "Don't be a smartass. Do they work?"

"Yeah."

"Guess your neck's not broken then. You should be more careful."

I slid up to a sitting position and gazed into her adorable face. "I do better when I'm not so distracted."

Her blues eyes bounced when she realized I was talking about her.

"I like your skirt."

"I like your quads."

"Wanna have coffee?"

"I shouldn't."

"You better. I gotta be under twenty-four hour observation, don't you think? In case of concussion."

"Well, how about twenty-four *minutes*."

Walking the few blocks to the coffee shop, we exchanged names and talked about people we both might know, mostly friends of friends on Facebook. "How do you like McClellan Prep?" I asked.

"Well, supposedly girls have a better chance of advancement if they don't have to compete with boys, but I think that's an outdated idea. Maybe without guys my school isn't rigorous enough. It's okay, free of distractions." She grinned up at me and nudged my arm.

Standing before the counter, she deliberated over pastry, her forefinger pressed into her chin, lips pursed, a girl who has a tough time making decisions. It gave me time to appreciate the finer things: her nice rack under the white uniform blouse, her back gracefully arched, which explained the kick to her skirt. I was ready to see her in pants, spandex preferably.

"Do you work out?" I asked.

"Only so I can eat this," she said, pointing to the chocolate croissant she had finally selected.

When we settled at a table, she asked, "What do you plan to specialize in?"

"Haven't got that far yet. Sports medicine, maybe."

"Heart for me. Or brain." She threw her palms up at her sides and rolled her eyes. "Right now I study twenty-four-seven so I can get into a good university."

Smart is sexy. I can go for a girl with purpose, who can stand on her own feet. I haven't got time for the clingy ones who text a hundred times a day: WHERE ARE YOU? WHY AREN'T YOU HANGING OUT WITH ME?

"You must do something besides study," I prompted.

"I fly."

"You're a pilot?"

"Uh-huh. I'm taking lessons. I just love it! The hell with tests and chem formulas! It's just the plane and the sky and me living in the moment!"

"That's how bike racing is for me."

"You race? Do you crash a lot?"

"Come on, now. I told you I had a perfectly good reason for that."

We were taking the same AP World Lit class, and we discussed Sartre. "'We make ourselves,'" she quoted. "I just love that. We choose our consequences at the same time we make our choices, or anyway, that's how I see it. What do you think?"

"*Possible* consequences. Just because we have free will doesn't mean we can control everything about our lives."

I'm fairly quiet in class, where the lit types think a discussion is a competition of put-downs, but it was fun to talk about these ideas with this Glory girl.

Half of her latte remained, but it had grown cold. She glanced at her silver watch and exclaimed, "Oh! Apparently, I *chose* to give up more studying time than I planned! I enjoyed talking with you, Evan."

"Same here, Glory."

"Good-bye." She extended her hand across the table. It was small, the nails not Elvira red and spiky but pearly and neatly trimmed. I recalled their touch on my neck. I wanted to kiss her, but I knew I'd have to work for that. My fingers closed around hers and held them so long, she began to gently tug away.

"May I have my hand back?"

"Oh, sorry, I wasn't done with it." I let her go and asked, "When can I see you?"

"I'm . . . well, I'm sorta with someone."

"Sorta? How does that work?"

"He's a family friend. We've known each other since we were two, and a few months ago we started dating, but I just wasn't feeling it, you know? I told him I wanted to be just friends again, but he talked me into staying together." A sad-sweet Mona Lisa smile formed on her lips. "He's a nice guy. I don't want to hurt him, but there's just no . . . sparks."

"Oh, there's gotta be sparks." I was feeling pretty sparky myself, and her wide blue eyes looking into mine seemed to indicate she was, too.

It drives me crazy when a girl is hard to get, not mercilessly

27

hard, but I like a challenge. I friended her on Facebook and checked out the competition: a preppy guy whose name begins with Alfred and ends with a Roman numeral three. Glory and I volleyed flirty texts back and forth. I asked her out a few times, but she put me off. Finally, I don't know if it was cycling over to her school at lunch and leaving a red rose beneath her windshield wiper or carving her name in a jack-o'-lantern and setting it aglow on her porch, but when her Harvest Dance rolled around, it wasn't old Alfred she invited. Ha! It was me!

Chapter Four

It's a big surprise the next morning at camp when Dashiell Shipley invites me to ride with him and his team. I only manage to hang with them early in the morning, when my legs are fresh. Tuesday I do a little better, but then Ben calls to say he needs me to go pick up some late-arriving riders at the airport.

Later that same afternoon I'm on the stepladder loading bikes onto the van's roof rack when I look down at Jay, who's handing me up the next bike, and I see Mike Townsend standing next to him.

"Evan, may we have a word with you?" Mike calls up to me.

"Sure." I secure the bike I'm working on and leap down.

"I'm wondering if you'd like to take part in a little study the team is conducting tomorrow," says Mike.

"Uh, sure," I answer, without even knowing what it is.

"Good. Meet us at the ASU Human Performance Lab at seven A.M."

"I've got—"

"Don't worry about being late for work. I've already cleared it with your boss."

"Okay, then. What sort of experiment?"

"VO2 max test. Ever taken one?"

"No."

"Then this ought to be very interesting. See you then."

"Awesome." This sort of test is expensive, and I never thought I'd get the chance to take one. VO2 max is short for maximal oxygen uptake, and it's the best indication of athletic ability and fitness in terms of cardiovascular capacity and aerobic power. While an average person will score 40 to 50 VO_2 max, professional cyclists are known to have much higher VO_2, especially Tour de France champions. Lance Armstrong once recorded an 85 VO_2 max, Miguel Indurain, an 88, and Greg LeMond, a 92.5 with a resting pulse of 32.

Wednesday morning I arrive at the HP Lab wearing cycling clothes. A technician seats me on a cycle ergometer, a stationary bicycle that measures work done by the athlete. There's another technician setting up the test, and a doctor standing by. Since the test takes the athlete to maximum workload, it's possible to go into cardiac arrest. A technician inserts a needle into my finger to take blood samples at certain intervals.

As soon as I'm all hooked up, the technician reports, "Resting pulse: forty-eight."

I start out spinning in a low gear to warm up. Once the

test starts, the workload becomes gradually harder as I'm told to increase my effort. Throughout the test oxygen inhaled and carbon dioxide exhaled is measured. By the time I'm pedaling to full capacity, sweat is pouring out of me as blood is drained from me. My head and heart are thumping, my legs are burning, and my chest is heaving.

At last, mercifully, I feel the gear becoming easier to push, and the technician tells me to gradually let up. Then comes the long, slow cooldown to protect my heart.

Once the results are in, Mike is beaming. "Congratulations, Evan. You scored a 78.8 VO_2 max. That's pretty damn good, but I'm going to expect an improvement."

I nod and thank him, wondering when I'm ever going to get another chance at a VO_2 max test. Not soon, I hope. It's agonizing.

I have to leave the lab to get to work, but I wish I could watch Dash, Bernard, Joris, and Dedrick take their tests. I wonder if I'll get to know their results. I'd love to compare them with mine.

On Thursday our local newspaper, the *Arizona Republic*, announces that Mike Townsend's pro cycling team has acquired not only one sponsor but two: Image Craft, a business for photographic services and display graphics, and Icon, a company specializing in themed environments. Now Townsend's team has a name: Image Craft–Icon. His Mercedes shows up at camp the same day covered in a cool blue graphic wrap with swirling white lines and the red Image Craft logo. Beneath that is the word Icon, with a gold *I* inside a black disk. The car wrap was fast work, but then that isn't surprising since that's a service Image Craft offers, with its company slogan, "Any image. Any size. Anywhere."

It's Sunday, the last day of the camp, and the ride is at South Mountain Park. We are grinding up a seven-mile, 2,300 foot climb, with several steep sections.

"Let's box Bernard in," says Dash. "Joris, take the front; Dedrick, to the left; and Evan, to the right."

As soon as we take our positions, Bernard begins to veer toward me, pushing me farther to the right, and when my front wheel rolls off the pavement, I let him ride through. He howls in laughter.

"Hold your line, Evan," instructs Dash.

We try it again, and Bernard immediately goes after me again. He presses his elbow again mine until I give him room to slip through.

"Ha!" shouts Bernard. "Sunny Boy is too damn timid for this business."

"You did better," Dash tells me, "but you've got to get used to the idea that this is a contact sport. In a tight pack you're going to knock into other riders, and if you're not assertive, they'll squeeze you out."

"Let's switch positions," says Bernard, and for one second I think I'm out of the hot seat.

"Same positions," insists Dash. "Go!"

This time Bernard attacks me even harder. We are elbow to elbow, forearm to forearm, then shoulder to shoulder. I'm able to hold him longer, but eventually he shoves me off the road again.

"Evan!" shouts Dash.

"I'm afraid I'll cause a crash."

"Bernard would be causing the crash, and it isn't likely, because probably he would go down, too." Dash rides alongside me, puts his arm around me, and squeezes my shoulder. "Come on, you can do this."

I wonder why it matters to him. Bernard is right. This drill would be doing their team a lot more good if he put Joris or Dedrick in my position.

We go at it again. This time when Bernard presses his shoulder against mine, I surge ahead, breaking the contact and forcing him to shift his weight to maintain balance. Now I'm just ahead of him, tight against Joris's rear wheel, and there's nowhere Bernard can go.

"Good job!" shouts Dash. "Now block me, Evan."

Panting, I ride up ahead of Dash and slow down. When he snakes around me, I sprint by him, take the front position, and slow down. We continue this way, approaching the cluster of radio towers at the summit.

Toward the top it's so steep, I feel like my crank arms or my legs are about to snap off. Finally at the finish, which dead-ends in a parking area, I take long slurps of sports drink and listen to my pounding heart rate gradually slow down. With the tremendous physical effort comes a wash of euphoria over my body. I guess it's nature's way of dealing with pain. Gazing out over the sweeping view of Phoenix, I think how relieved I am that this is the last day of this torturous riding, but I'm also elated that I got to spend it with Dash Shipley. Who would believe that such a famous pro would bother giving a rookie like me a few pointers?

We descend the mountain and roll to the parking lot around eleven-thirty. Many of the cyclists are loading up their bikes to head in for lunch. Others turn around to make another go at the mountain. I'm surprised to find out that Dash expects me to be one of those riders. My legs are wet noodles. I tell him I've got duties to attend to, but Mike assures me that it's fine with Ben that I ride with his team some more.

"Pace me up the mountain," Dash orders me. "Let's see what you've got left."

The whole team turns around, Dash glued to my wheel. By now there's a stiff headwind. A team usually shares the workload by forming a paceline. The rider in front bucks the wind for a time, veers to the left, coasts to the rear of the line, and the second person takes his pull.

When I try to peel off the front, Dash says, "Stay where you are, Evan, and speed it up."

I have to rise out of my saddle and dance the bike up the incline. I settle down again, but it isn't long before Dash says, "Push it, Evan! You're fading. Come on, man. Only four miles to go."

Alongside of us glides the team car, displaying the logos of their new sponsors Image Craft and Icon. Rainier quietly observes us and occasionally makes notes on his clipboard.

During the last steep mile Dash, Bernard, Joris, Dedrick, and many of the riders on other teams pass me, then drop me. I stand on the pedals, my chest heaving.

When I get to the summit, Dash pats me on the back. "I know that was bad, but don't worry. You'll get stronger."

I nod like I actually believe him.

After lunch camp breaks up. I shower in the employees' room and change into jeans and an Arizona Cycling Tours T-shirt. Ben gives me all sorts of odd jobs: packing equipment, loading vans, transporting the riders' luggage. At one point I sit down and can hardly get up again. Other times when I'm standing, one knee buckles or both legs start to shake. I imagine being home in my own bathtub, soaking in the hottest water I can stand.

When nearly all the riders, vans, cars, and trailers have cleared out, I get a request to visit room 315. I wonder if Dash Shipley is being nice enough to say good-bye or maybe it's Mike Townsend offering me a tip for my services.

When Mike invites me into their suite, I find Bernard sprawled out on the sofa having a beer, Rainier going over some paperwork at the table, and Dash talking on his phone.

"Sure, Princess," he says. "Let me just say hi to the kids." He pauses, then exclaims in a high-pitched, excited voice. "Hello, Queenie! . . . What's that? . . . Oh, Daddy's riding his bike. We'll have another tea party soon as I get home. . . Uh-huh, promise. Let me talk to Logan, okay?" After another pause he lowers his voice, saying, "Hey, tough guy. How'd basketball practice go today?"

Mike motions for me to sit at the table with him and Rainier. Dash hangs up and comes over. My heart is thumping, thumping, thumping, and I don't know why.

"Do you want to do the talking or should I?" Mike asks Dash.

"You tell him, Mike."

"We've decided to—"

"How would you like to ride for us in the Tour of California?" Dash blurts.

I say the thing most appropriate for the situation: "Uh," and then my mouth sort of hangs open for a while before I add, "You're joking."

"No joke," says Mike. He slides over the papers Rainier has been going over. "The contract is right here."

I look at Dash, and he grins back at me with his mighty white teeth. "You proved yourself on the mountain this morning."

Bernard sits upright on the sofa and yanks his big nose. "That's odd. I could have sworn Sunny Boy *didn't* prove himself."

"Now, Bernie, it was a tough climb at a hard pace," says Dash. "He only faded on the last mile."

"The TOC is seven hundred miles," says Bernard, as if any of us needs a reminder.

"Who says he has to last the whole race?" Dash knocks my shoulder with his palm, which prompts me to close my mouth. "Say something, would ya, Evan?"

"Uh . . . wow!" How can I afford to miss that much school? What will Glory think? How will I talk my parents into letting me go? Why me and not another pro? "Are you sure you want *me*?"

"No," says Rainier flatly. "I am against this." He looks at Mike. "You are sending in a boy to do a man's work."

"We've already talked about this," Mike tells him.

"Look here, Evan. I'll show you what I'm thinking," says Dash. Not *we*, but *I*. So it's mainly Dash who wants me. He shuffles through some papers on the table and comes up with a map of California with the eight stages of the race marked on it. "Stage One is a time trial in Sacramento, only twelve miles. You can handle that, right?"

"I've never ridden a time trial bike." As exciting as this is, it feels wrong, like I'm in over my head. But if Dash Shipley thinks I can do this, why shouldn't I think so, too?

"You'll get a couple of days to get used to the bike, and Rainier will give you a few pointers. Basically, it's just put your head down and go! Now, Stage Two is the road race from Davis to Santa Rosa. It's a tough course, over a hundred miles, and there's some serious climbing at the end, but you can just sit in all day and rest."

I nod. He makes it sound like keeping up with a peloton of pros is easy.

"Then comes Stage Three from Sausalito to Santa Cruz— that's where I need you." With his forefinger he traces the route down the coast of California. "There'll be groups of riders breaking away all day down Highway One, but they probably won't include the serious competition. The real race won't heat up until the last climb, up Bonny Doon. That's where you come in. You and a couple of other riders are gonna pace me up the climb and on to the finish line in Santa Cruz. You can give it all you've got because after that, you're done! You can abandon, having served the team well, and I should gain enough time to put me in the yellow jersey for the rest of the race."

" 'Ah, the best laid plans of mice and men . . . ,' " quotes Bernard, squeezing one eye shut to peer into his empty beer bottle.

"Shut up, Bernie!" says Dash. "Remember, when we decided to start our own team, one of our goals was to develop young talent."

"Yeah, but not this young, not for one stage of one race," says Rainier. "This is a mistake."

"We came to this camp looking for young riders to recruit, and Evan is the best unattached climber we found," argues Dash.

Bernard just shakes his beefy head. He hasn't showered yet, and the sweat and grime of the road has caused his woolly hair to stick out in all directions.

"It's true that time is running out," says Mike. "The TOC is only five weeks away. Plus the president of Image Craft is mighty pleased we're including a rider from Phoenix on our roster. Now that we have sponsors to issue paychecks, Salvatore Netti and Charles Larocque have signed contracts as well." Mike turns to me. "Larocque is a Canadian sprinter, in case you don't know."

"And a good friend of mine in France knows of able, out-of-work domestiques," says Rainier. "We can engage one of them."

Dash adds, "Right. So we need one more climber—Evan."

"And when the Tour de France rolls around in July, we'll have another dozen handpicked riders on our roster," says Mike. "For now, we're going to rely on Evan here. This young man is going to ride his heart out for us on Stage Three, and then—*poof*—he'll be gone, back to . . . What is it young guys like yourself do in this desert?"

"Uh, finish high school?"

"Good, you do that—finish high school."

Is this really happening? My mom just might kill me now. "I . . . have a question."

"Sure, go ahead," says Mike. "Ask us anything."

"Could I maybe ride more stages?"

"Of course!" says Dash. "Hang in as long as you can."

"I'd like to finish," I say wistfully.

"Finish! What the hell for?" blurts Bernard. "You enter a bike race to win or help a teammate win, or blow up trying. Finish! What good is that?"

Voices of Arizona Cycling Tours guests echo in my mind. Finishing for the sake of finishing is a tourist's way of thinking, and now I needed to develop a racer's mentality. Bernard is rude, but I can learn from him.

Rainier stands up, hovering over me. "Take off your shirt."

I just look at him.

He flutters his hand impatiently. "Come on, come on. Let's have a look at you."

I stand and lift my shirt over my head.

"Five feet six?"

I nod. I like to think I'm five seven, but I know I'm somewhere in-between.

"About sixty-eight kilos?"

I try to do the math in my head, but can't think straight. "One hundred fifty-two pounds," I say.

"It's what I thought," says Rainier. "You'll need to lose five to seven pounds." He pinches my pecs, making me wince. "You go to the gym? Work the upper body?" He makes a motion as if he's bench-pressing.

"Uh-huh."

"Cut it out. Going up the mountain, you don't need to carry any extra weight here." He slaps my chest hard enough to sting.

"Weightlifting is a part of my PE class, and my teacher is the football coach, and—"

"You need a note from your *directeur sportif*?" Rainier asks sarcastically.

"I'll handle it." Refusing to lift could cause me to flunk PE. I'll have to fake it. Coach Brenner has probably never heard of a *directeur sportif*. I'm sure he thinks bike racing is for the French, whom he would call sissy frogs.

I put my shirt back on, sit down, and Mike slides the contract in front of me, setting a pen next to it. "Are you eighteen?"

"Yeah, my birthday was in November."

"Perfect. You can sign without parental consent. You also have two weeks to change your mind or have your folks change your mind for you. Here, it says so right here: Clause Twelve."

I've been taught to read something before I sign it, so I do. "This is a one-year contract," I say.

"Oh, yes," says Mike, "same as all the other riders have. Note Clause Five. You can get out of it at any point in time with mutual consent. You already have my consent to leave after Stage Three of the TOC in February."

"Five weeks!" I gasp. "That's such a short time to get ready."

"True," said Rainier. "You must go on—what do you call it—home study?"

"That's for sick kids in my school district. I wouldn't qualify."

"It doesn't matter," says Dash. "Already I see Evan's dedication. And Rainier will have him on the bike every minute he's not in school or asleep."

"Oh! I'm going on a snowboarding trip with my girlfriend's family the MLK weekend."

Rainier shakes his head. "No, you are not. In three days you can ride four hundred miles, maybe five."

"But I can't just disappoint my girlfriend like that!"

"Get used to disappointing your girlfriend a lot if you're going into this business," says Bernard.

I think of all the other things I like to do besides riding. I'm not "going into this business," as Bernard puts it. I'm riding one totally amazing race, *part* of one.

"Anyway, snowboarding is out of the question." Mike taps the contract with the end of his pen. "Clause Fifteen: . . . no dangerous activities that could cause injury."

"All right." I take up my copy of the contract and try to read through all the legal jargon word for word, but my eyes glaze over. Just as I'm about to sign, I notice an amount of money that makes my eyes pop. Oh, yeah, "professional" means getting paid. My signature comes out as shaky as a little old man's.

Out the door, I can't wait to tell Glory. I still have lots to do on the job for Ben, so I just text her, "I'M A PROFESSIONAL CYCLIST."

She immediately texts back, "WHAT'S THAT MEAN?"

I realize, number one, I shouldn't have told her that way. Number two, I've got a lot of explaining to do, and not just to Glory.

Chapter Five

Ah, the green stuff! Mom makes a huge batch every year and freezes it in packets to use year-round. The basil is from our backyard. She carries it in by the armloads, and the whole house fills up with its smell. She grinds it in the food processor with plenty of pine nuts and olive oil, then heaps it on plates of pasta. You can't get pesto like this in restaurants; theirs is usually only a few green flecks scattered around and a couple nuts ground so fine, they don't even crunch.

Pesto and pasta, a loaf of sourdough, and Caesar salad, the best recovery meal there is—it's what Mom has waiting for me when I come home from my last day of camp. Pasta is the preferred food of cyclists, even served for breakfast during long stage races. I bend over my plate to shorten the distance my fork has to travel and shovel it in. I better enjoy it while I can. When I tell my news to my parents, all hell will break lose.

Glory isn't enthused about it. After I finished work, I called to give her the details. She congratulated me and asked a few questions, but she doesn't understand what a big deal this is. She thinks cycling is just my job and what I do for exercise.

I'm deep in thought as I plow through my pesto and pasta. It's just the three of us at dinner; Meredith has returned to college.

"Aren't you going to have a little, Connie?" Dad asks.

I look over at Mom's empty plate. She's nibbling on a piece of bread, no butter. "It doesn't agree with me."

"It's really good, Mom. It's my favorite."

"I know, Ren. I wish I could enjoy it like you."

"You've been awfully quiet about camp," says Dad.

"Hungry," I say, my mouth full.

"Did you get to say good-bye to Dash?" he asks.

I nod and keep inhaling my food.

"Let him eat," says Mom. "There are some terrific after-holiday sales going on. I got you a couple of pairs of heavy socks for your Colorado trip, Ren."

I look at her a bit sadly. "I'm not going."

Her eyes widen. "You and Glory had a fight?"

I shake my head, still eating.

"Her parents canceled?"

I push my plate aside. "I've been given a chance to ride in the Tour of California."

"What?" they exclaim together.

I talk real fast, telling them about everything: taking the VO_2 test, riding with the Image Craft–Icon team, going over Dash's plans for me in the third stage, and, finally, signing the contract.

Dad's eyes and mouth are like three round gold coins, reflecting my excitement. "You could win the white jersey, Ren!"

Laughing, I hold up both palms. "It's for the *fastest* rider under twenty-three, not the *youngest.*"

"No! No! No!" Mom shouts. "This so-called contract is invalid. You can't sign anything without us."

"I'm eighteen," I say quietly.

"I don't care how old you are," says Mom. "As long as you are under this roof, you'll do as we say."

I look at Dad. Mom looks at Dad. He clears his throat, but it seems his words don't come readily. "Wh-what about school, Ren?"

"I'll only miss a few days."

"Long enough for your grades to go in the toilet," snaps Mom. "What about graduation?"

My high school has a rule to prevent seniors from ditching: if we miss more than eight days of class, then we can't walk with our class. I've already been absent four days because of a nasty flu. "I've thought about that, Mom. I'll probably miss only three school days, four at the most."

She's shaking her head. "You're not going, Evan. That's final."

I don't argue. The worst is over. I broke my news and it's going to take awhile to sink in. But I am racing, and Mom can't stop me. She just doesn't know it yet.

One Sunday, Dad and I cycle out to Pinnacle Peak, a moderate ride for him, a recovery ride for me. Each week Rainier emails me a workout schedule. Every day I have to email him back, reporting how much of the workout I was able to complete, my speed, pulse, how I felt, and so on. No matter how hard I try, I can never do enough. Rainier always expects more, more, more!

I'm training so hard, my legs ache all the time, but it's really true that an easy day feels better on the muscles than a day completely off. The Pinnacle Peak ride is a forty-two-mile loop from our house, heading out to the desert beyond North Scottsdale. The ride is mostly flat, with a gradual seven-mile climb in the middle.

There's not much traffic, and the shoulder is wide enough to ride side by side. Dad wears one of those dorky little mirrors on a wire that attaches to his glasses. Relying on those things are like asking for death because of the blind spots, but Dad is forced to use one because of his neck injury, which makes it necessary to twist his shoulders to see behind him. The accident that caused that injury is the reason Mom hates bikes so much.

When I was just two and Meredith was four, Dad was out riding alone when a pickup's side mirror smacked him in the shoulder. He flew off his bike, slid across the desert on his belly, and came to a halt when his head slammed into a rock, cracking his helmet into two neat halves. The driver of the pickup sped away, leaving Dad for dead.

Dad woke up in a hospital bed, with nearly his whole body in traction. At first it seemed he was going to be a quadriplegic, but over six months he gradually learned to walk again. When it became apparent that he would be nearly 100 percent rehabilitated, Mom went ballistic. "You nearly left me a widow with two babies to raise on my own!" she accused. He agreed not to ride again, a promise he kept for over fifteen years.

I'm glad to have him to ride with now. I rise out of the saddle to sprint up a little incline, and Dad notices me wince.

"This won't be like amateur racing, you know," he says. "It's the pros, and it's going to be brutal."

"I know."

"Okay, so you'll make it through the time trial in Sacramento, but then there's Davis to Santa Rosa, a long way at a fierce pace. Maybe you won't be able to keep up with the peloton. Maybe you won't make the time cut, and you're out of the race."

"I know, Dad." Doesn't he realize I lie awake nights worrying about this?

I surge ahead to take the front position, and we continue in single file, so it's hard to talk. At Pinnacle Peak Park we stop to rest and refill our water bottles. We sit on a rock bench and gaze out at the peak, this gigantic hunk of granite jutting out of the desert. It's peaceful here, a slight breeze cooling our sweaty bodies.

"Do you understand why they signed you on?" Dad blurts.

"To help out on the third stage, like Dash said."

"But does it make sense?"

I sigh. I thought this was going to be a sweet little recovery ride, my dad and I bonding over the sport we both love, but no. It's turning into another grilling session.

When I don't reply, Dad continues. "It seems like they're just using you. They'll chew you up and spit you out, and it won't mean a thing to them."

I laugh a single ha! in exasperation. "Then let them chew me up and spit me out. It sounds like one hell of an experience to me. Why so negative, Dad?"

"I'm worried about you, Ren. Something about offering a kid a pro contract doesn't set right with me. Do you realize the racing will be the easy part? There's the media, the pressure to win, the wheeling and dealing. They may even force you to take drugs."

"Dad, Dad! Who's they?"

"I don't know. There's allegations against Dash."

"That's because he's a tour champion, and everyone wants

to take down the guy on top. He's never failed a drug test. That means he's clean."

"Or he's got a good masking agent."

I let out a puff of air and stare out at the peak. "He wouldn't risk it."

"Oh, no? Your definition of a champion is some kind of hero. My definition is one who's willing to risk everything. When a three-week race is decided within seconds, the guy who wins is the one willing to take something for a little extra go-power, legal or not."

I just shake my head. "This is about Mom, isn't it? She's been after you about this. I thought you were on my side."

"There's no *sides,* Ren. Both Mom and I have reservations."

"Right. The unified front. If you had a chance to be in a big race like this at my age, you would've jumped at the chance, just like what I'm doing."

"I'm afraid you're too young for this, too naive."

"There's fourteen-year-olds in the Olympics."

"With their parents right at their sides."

Oh, hell. Now I see where this discussion is headed. I shake my head. "No, Dad."

He talks faster. "I've already checked with my supervisor. I can get the time off. I'm going to California with you."

"No, Dad."

"Hear me out, Ren. I'll just be on the sidelines, in the background, in case you need—"

"I signed a contract as an adult. I'd feel completely different if you were there, like I can't handle it. It would shake my confidence."

"But if you get seriously injured or—it's not even that. I'm worried you'll get lost in all the hoopla and forget who you really are."

"I don't even know what that means." I lurch from the bench and seize my bike.

He grasps my handlebars. "Wait, Ren. Calm down."

"You're not going to California."

We stare into each other's faces. The tension causes muscle spasms beneath the scar tissue on his neck. I've hurt his feelings, but I couldn't help it.

I wait for him to get his bike, and we ride out of the park. I pour my anger into cranking the pedals. A couple of times I look behind me, see that I've dropped him, and wait for him. When he catches up, we don't speak.

One night I wake up parched. I can't seem to drink enough for the amount I'm training, even though it's winter. I have a choice to cross the hall and get tap water from the bathroom or go downstairs and get cold, sweet water from the dispenser. I decide the latter is worth the effort.

In the dim light from the stove top, I think I see my grandfather's ghost, dressed in a bathrobe, sitting at the kitchen table and sipping Chianti from a jelly jar. It's not Nonno, who lived with us his last couple of years, but Mom. I wish I had stayed upstairs. I don't want to have to deal with her now.

Whenever she can't sleep, she sips a glass of wine to make her sleepy, just like her father used to do. Stress only exacerbates her condition, and as I watch her doubled over, clutching her abdomen, I feel guilty.

"Are you okay, Mom?"

She raises her head, startled. "What are you doing up, Ren?"

"Just thirsty," I say, reaching for a glass from the cupboard.

"Sit with me a moment."

"It's late, Mom." I know I don't want to hear what she has to say. Like, I'm done with confiding in her about girls. When

I brought this girl Melissa home, she said, "Looks like she has hot pants. Don't get her pregnant. It will ruin your life." That made me think she'd approve of Glory. "Very prim and proper" was Mom's opinion of her when I dared to ask. "Just don't get too attached," she warned me. Gee, thanks, Mom.

I pour myself some water and take the chair opposite her. "You look like Nonno sitting there."

"I was thinking of my own nonno—your great-grandfather—Charles Graifemberg. He emigrated from Italy, you know. I just happened to remember he rode the Tour de France."

"Really? What year?"

She shrugs. "Late thirties."

"Oh! It was so wicked then! A lot of the roads weren't even paved. Those guys had to climb the Alps in mud. How'd he do?"

"I don't know. The record books only hold the winners, right?"

"Still, it's a great story. I'd like to know more about him."

Abruptly, Mom's face crumbles. "I'm not going to get to see my only son walk with his class."

"Mom, I'll probably only miss a few days."

"I know you, Evan. You'll want to finish the race."

Actually, I'm not sure how many days of school I'll miss due to preparations, traveling, and racing. Missing graduation is a very real possibility. It would suck not to celebrate with my friends, then come around to school to pick up my diploma the next day. "It's not really fair," I say. "Football players miss lots of class, but participating in a school sport doesn't count as missing instruction time."

"You know I'm dead set against this bike-racing business. Look what biking did to your dad. You're damn lucky you ever got to know him. Please, Ren, for my sake, call up Mr. Townsend and tell him you've changed your mind."

I'm amazed how much resistance she's putting up. By now, I thought she'd accept it. My parents are usually not the type to forbid their kids from doing stuff. They reason with Meredith and me, they offer their guidance, but then they often let us do what we want. Like Meredith was against attending UA or ASU, even though that's all our parents can afford. She applied to Yale, Brown, Harvard, several of the University of California campuses, and when each rejection letter arrived, she would lie on her bed and cry and moan that she was "dumb" and "not good enough" and make everyone in the family miserable. When UC Santa Barbara finally accepted her, she snatched up the opportunity to attend, knowing that she was burdening our parents with out-of-state tuition and unnecessary student loans. I remember the sort of frozen look Mom had on her face when Meredith announced her decision, and that's just how she looks at me now.

"It will be okay, Mom. I'll make up my schoolwork when I get back."

"I know how easily you get sidetracked, Ren. Remember, on the way to karate, you saw a sign for drum lessons, so you just had to do that. Then it was computers." She groans horribly, tenses, then rocks forward when another attack seizes her body.

I touch her shoulder. "I'm real worried about you, Mom. Dad is, too."

When the attack subsides, she murmurs, "I'll be fine. I bet it's an ulcer. Let's talk about you. When I saw your SAT score was two hundred points higher than Meredith's, my eyes nearly popped out of my head. I thought, Everything comes easy for this boy. He learns quickly, doesn't freeze up on tests. He's got what it takes to go all the way to MD."

"I will, Mom. I'll do it."

"Promise me you'll only miss three days of school."

"Uh, I can't do that. I'll have to see."

Mom drops her face into her hand, making me feel like shit.

I drain my glass and stand. "How many years did Great-Grandfather Charles ride the Tour de France?"

She looks up. "Just once as far as I know. The Tour riders in those days were just ordinary laborers. He left off laying bricks to ride in the Tour, and the day after it was over, he went back to laying bricks."

"That's how it will be with me, Mom. You'll see. After one ride in the Tour of California, I'll be right back here laying bricks."

She smiles weakly.

I hug her good-night. "Don't worry so much. It's not good for you." Walking out of the kitchen, I turn back to her. "My SATs were two hundred points higher than Meredith's, really?"

"Did I say that? Don't you dare tell her I told you."

Chapter Six

Dinner at the Albrights'. We sit in high-backed chairs listening to tinkling piano music as I wonder which fork to use for the spinach-pecan-pear salad. Their North Scottsdale house has it all: panoramic views, vaulted ceilings, fancy furnishings, and monster floral arrangements. Classy but not comfortable, not like a real home.

The truth is Glory's folks are not my favorite people to hang out with. They're civil to me, but I get the vibe they don't think I'm good enough. They're both athletic and tan, but as old as grandparents. Once upon a time they had a son, Robert Hunter, much older than Glory, who died in a sailing accident. The sadness of this tragedy haunts the family.

"Everything looks great, Mrs. Albright," I say.

She turns her gray, watery eyes on me. Glory told me she has had plastic surgery, but bitterness is sunk deep into her face even though the wrinkles have been smoothed away. "It's too bad you won't be joining us at our place in Aspen, Evan. It's stunning in winter."

Even though I've apologized a couple of times, I try again. "Sorry, Mrs. Albright. I wish I were going. I know it's rude to cancel out."

"Not to worry," Mr. Albright says with a hollow cheerfulness. He made his fortune in the mining business. He has a full head of gray hair, cropped short like a bristle brush. "We were able to engage some old friends."

"Even though it was rather impromptu, Bob," says Mrs. Albright. "The Thorntons no doubt surmised they were second choice."

"Nonsense, Marianne. We're too good friends to fuss about propriety. Be glad they can make it. We'll have a foursome for bridge, and Glory Beth will have company on the slopes."

I realize who the Thorntons are just as I'm trying to swallow. A pecan gets lodged in my gullet, so that Mr. Albright gives me a hearty slap on the back. I gulp down water as I glare across the rim of my goblet at Glory. Her eyes dart away from mine, and she blushes.

I'm forced to sit through three more courses before I can get her off alone on a walk around the neighborhood. As soon as we've passed a few houses, I start yelling. "No! No! No! You're not going on that snowboarding trip. You've got to get out of it. Fake the flu or something."

Glory tries to laugh it off. "You're crazy. Of course I'm going."

"You're not sleeping under the same roof as Alfred!"

"Oh, that."

"Yes, that. When were you going to get around to telling me about that?"

She shrugs. "It's no big deal."

"The hell it's not!" I pick up a rock and fling it into the ravine behind the houses.

"Calm down, Evan. Our families have been going on trips together for years. He's like a cousin."

"A kissing cousin?"

"You're not being fair! You were the one who canceled out on me!"

"And this is payback?"

"You know my parents made these plans."

"Oh, they've got plans! Throw you and Alfred together for the long weekend. At least Alfred Alexander Thornton the third is good enough to jump into the sack with their golden girl."

Glory stops and crosses her arms. "He's respectful. He's kind. He'd never yell at me and say such horrible things." She turns and struts toward home.

What a damn fool I am! Pushing her into Mr. Nice Guy's arms. "Glory, wait!" I run past her to block her path. She's crying. I made her cry. I want to put my life on rewind, go back and make it all right between us. I want to accept the Albrights' invitation to Aspen and—what? Not sign on for the TOC? I press my forehead against hers, imagining her and Alfred tumbling in the snow together, cuddling by the fire. It kills me. I grip her shoulders and moan, "I can't stand it. I've seen him on Facebook, and he's a good-looking guy."

"I don't want him. I want you."

"Oh, Glory, do you have to go?"

She presses her lips into a tight little smile and cocks her head in an adorable way. "Believe me, you can trust me with Alfred."

But can I trust him with her?

When we get back to her porch, I run my hands up and down her arms. "Sorry for being an asshole. Do you forgive me, babe?"

She tilts her chin for a kiss. The front door opens, and Mr. Albright sticks his head out. "Can I have a word with you, Evan?"

Glory and I look at each other. Her eyebrows arch to indicate she doesn't know what this is about, either.

We go inside, and Mr. Albright leads me to his den. He's got a tricky hip which goes out every once in a while. Tonight he's hobbling along, using a five iron as a cane. It takes a long time to go through several rooms, down a long hall, and up a winding staircase. The whole time I'm thinking about movies I've seen where a disgruntled father takes out a checkbook and asks how much it will cost him for the guy to never see his daughter again.

We finally arrive in his den. It has a great view of the desert, same as the rest of the house, but it's obvious Mrs. Albright hasn't been allowed in for interior decorating. The shelves are crowded with golfing trophies. The walls are plastered with photos of sailboats and the sea. Heaped high, one on top of the other, are model sailboats in glass cases, some as big as three by four feet.

I stand in front of a large clipper and admire its craftsmanship. "Wow, you made all these? How'd you do it?"

"Lots of patience. Life is long, and I was forced to retire early. I've had to fill my time doing something besides playing golf."

I stare at a photo of a guy about my age, with Glory's face.

He's wearing a captain's hat and leaning against a sailboat. It's easy to figure out who he is.

Mr. Albright comes over and looks on with me. "Our son, Hunter. Died in a sailing accident."

"I'm sorry. Glory told me."

"Hell of a kid." Mr. Albright is a little, muscled man, and tension causes his shoulders to rise to his ears. "A squall came up; the boom shifted suddenly. He lost his balance and got cracked in the skull. He was racing America's Junior Cup at the time, and winning." He jerks his head toward me. "What about you? Are you going to win the Tour of California?" I spot the glint in his eye that signals he's teasing.

"I'm going to try to help Dash Shipley win. He's formed a new American team."

"Yes, I read about it in the paper. I know the guy who started Image Craft. Built the business from the ground up. Good man."

"I know." Since I signed the contract the team has toured the Image Craft facilities and met its founder, Doug Olson. He and his wife, Penney, used to race bikes and cycle-tour Europe extensively. He even built bicycle frames at one time.

"Do you think Shipley can win?" Mr. Albright asks me.

"Yeah, I do. Do you follow bicycle racing?"

"I know something about nearly every sport." He nods at a huge flat-screen TV mounted behind his desk. "I look at that thing quite a lot."

"You must also spend a lot of time golfing." I nod toward his trophies. "Looks like you're good at it."

"Not bad. When the hip behaves. It seems ridiculous, really. Grown men chasing after a little white ball. Not too exciting. No risk. Doesn't get the heart rate up like sailing. We left Huntington Beach after the accident, sold the boats. Marianne couldn't stand the sight of the sea, so we moved to this desert to be close to her folks. At the time, I wondered how we could possibly bear our loss, but of course, we had our Glory Beth to think about. Your race will be televised, I presume."

"Yes, sir."

"Good. I'll be watching." He is again drawn to the photo of his son. "Hunter died doing what he loved."

I get the feeling he is telling me something else, what none of my family members or Glory have said. He seems to understand why I have to race the TOC. "Thanks for . . . thanks for the talk, Mr. Albright. I guess I better be going."

"One other thing: how serious are you about our daughter?" He leans in to me, our faces so close, it takes all my willpower not to step away. I'm tempted to take the easy way out, tell him we *care* about each other. Instead, I blurt the truth: "We're in love."

"Ah." He presses his tongue against his lower lip, raises his face to the ceiling, then abruptly glares at me. "That was quick. And that means . . . ?"

What a question! "It means . . . well, we want to be together and—"

"Do you know Glory Beth has a four point two seven GPA and a near-perfect SAT score?"

"We've never discussed scores."

"Do you know it's a distinct possibility she'll be accepted to Harvard?"

"I know she's applied."

"Will you be accepted to Harvard?" he asks pointedly.

"No, sir. But I've got ten years of college ahead of me, same as Glory."

"UA, I hear."

"It's a good medical school. It turns out MDs as well as Harvard."

"Not quite as well," he says. "Now Gloria is making noises

about UA, too, since she met you. You wouldn't want to hold her back, would you?"

"Of course not." He doesn't seem to understand Glory wants to stick around Arizona for his and his wife's sake more than mine, but it's not my place to clue him in. My answer seems to satisfy him because he smiles, or at least tries to. "Good luck in that bicycle race of yours."

He sinks into his leather chair and takes up a magazine, leaving me to wind my way back to the front of the house on my own. I'm greeted by Mrs. Albright, who tells me Glory has already "retired" to her studies.

Outside, wheeling my bike down the sloping drive, I sneak a peek through the window of the Albrights' partially subterranean gym. Glory is in workout capris, walking on the treadmill while peering into a gigantic textbook. She reminds me of one of her dad's boats, trapped in its case. I want to bust her out. I kneel on one knee and tap on the glass. She leaps off the treadmill and lopes over to crack the window.

"What'd he want?"

I shrug. "He asked about the race."

"That's it?"

"He talked about your brother."

"Oh. I think you remind Daddy of Hunter. I think you've really won him over."

"You think?"

She nods happily.

"'Night, babe. Don't study too late."

She kisses her fingertip and presses it against the glass.

Chapter Seven

A cold front comes into Phoenix MLK weekend, but still I'm on the bike six to eight hours, all three days. Those are some long, lonely miles to think about Glory in Aspen with Alfred. I'm not entirely alone. Jay is driving SAG for me in a borrowed Arizona Cycling Tours van. When I get to shivering too much, I jump into the van, change my sweat-drenched clothes for dry ones, and sit awhile in front of the heater before going out again.

On one break I get a photo sent to my phone from Glory, her cheeks rosy against her furry cap. I show it to Jay.

"Sweet."

All weekend she's been sending flirty texts and cute photos, trying to reassure me. "Do you think Alfred is Harvard bound, too?"

Jay's black brows have a train wreck over his nose. "Those preppy boys definitely have a leg up."

"Dude, you're not helping!"

Glory comes back to me, and everything is great between us, except that I don't see much of her in the next three weeks. I'm on the bike as much as possible and studying hard, knowing I'll fall behind while I'm in California. I've given up trying to read while lying down. I fall asleep sitting up, even when I'm trying to pay attention in class.

I have to be a pro cyclist on the inside and a high school kid on the outside. The newspaper reported my signing with Image Craft–Icon and riding the TOC, but few people said anything about it to me. The guys in my bike club congratulated me, of course, and they work hard to support me on my training rides, but I don't say much about it at school. Most kids don't know competitive sports outside of school even exist.

I stop at the school office, and the attendance lady tells me what I already know: my absences will be unexcused. I go around to all my teachers to get the work I'll miss. In AP World Lit I'm assigned Dante's *Inferno*. That ought to be fun to plow through while riding the TOC, two kinds of hell.

Thursday, the night before I'm scheduled to fly into Sacramento to join the Image Craft–Icon team, I take Glory out for chicken bowls at a fast-food Japanese place. We don't have much time. I have to get home so Jay can pick me up to supposedly go to the movies, while I know he's really taking me to a surprise going-away party my bike club is throwing me.

"How do you act surprised when you're not?" I ask Glory. "Isn't it too obvious to even pretend?"

"I guess." Jay is always in a hurry, and I know when he

set up the event on Facebook, he clicked the whole bike club network rather than individual names.

We eat in silence for a few minutes. Glory, it seems, has something on her mind. I wonder if she's feeling sad about my leaving.

I reach over and give her hand a quick squeeze. "Hey."

"I've got something to talk to you about."

I hate conversations that start this way. They're never good.

"Don't blow up on me."

"Okay." My heart beats faster.

She takes a deep breath. "Well, this Saturday is Bishop Prep's Sweetheart Ball."

"And you're *my* sweetheart."

She holds up her palm. "This guy I know rented a limo for four couples, and this girl's mom is making dinner. They're part of a bunch of kids I hang out with. My mom says kids today don't date, they swarm."

"We date."

"Evan!"

"Okay."

"The dance is going to be totally bomb. The guys have to wear all white and the girls all red. It will look so pretty, and I already have a red dress I've worn only once, at last year's winter formal." She pauses, checking me out, but I don't say anything. "One guy's date bailed last minute—mono or drug rehab, something, I didn't get the whole story—and he asked me if I'd fill in, go with him as a *friend*, and I'm not gonna lie, it's Alfred."

I try for an even tone. "And you accepted?"

"No. I told him I would check with the boyfriend." She points her forefingers at me, thumbs up like six-shooters. "It's not worth it if you're going to go all crazy on me."

Noooooooooo! Cut that guy out of your life or I'm going to have to tear him a new one! I hope my grimace looks more like a grin. "It sounds like a lot of fun. You should go."

"Really?"

"Why not? While I'm off on my great California adventure I can't expect you to sit at home."

She's happy and obviously relieved. I feel a little sick. On the way out to the car, she pauses to give me a big hug and a long, sexy kiss in front of the whole world.

"How low-cut is that red dress?" I ask.

She extends her forearm across her front. "About . . ." She slowly lowers it to a daring level.

"Oh, hell."

"You act like my dad."

"Worse. I'm the boyfriend." She laughs, but I'm not a happy camper. I can't stand the thought of Alfred staring at her tits all night. "You'll send me a picture, won't you?"

"Sure."

"Just of you."

She giggles. "I know."

When I drop Glory off at her house, we linger in the car over our good-bye. It will be the longest time we've ever been apart.

"I'll miss you," she says.

"Me, too."

She strokes my cheek. "Be safe."

"I will. I'll text you when I get to California."

"Okay." Her hand drifts toward the door handle.

"Oh, wait! Uh . . . here." From my jacket pocket I withdraw a small package wrapped in white tissue paper and a red bow and thrust it into her hand. "Happy Valentine's Day."

"Oh, Evan! Now I feel bad. I figured since we wouldn't be together on Valentine's Day, we wouldn't be exchanging."

"It's nothing," I say, even though it took me a long time to find and it cost a lot.

"Do you want me to open it now?"

"No!" Suddenly I'm embarrassed by its contents. "Save it for Monday. Sorry we won't be together."

"Me, too."

After one more good-bye kiss, I watch her run up the porch steps, pause, and turn back. She leaps into the car—nearly into my lap—and bores her face into my chest. When she lifts it, she's crying.

"You'll come back to me in one piece?"

"Oh, babe."

"You won't fly off a cliff or something?"

"Hey, now." I stroke her hair.

"I was only four when Hunter died, but I remember him. I remember my parents explaining how I'd never see him again." Fresh tears surface, and I hold her tight. At last she wipes her eyes and gives me a weak smile. "Well, you're not very good at holding the bike upright."

"Not true!" I say, and we laugh together.

I don't take Glory's advice and do act surprised at the party. Of course, I fool no one, and all the guys give Jay a good razzing for sending me an invitation to my own surprise party. There's plenty of good laughs. The party seems to be just getting started when I beg off and ask Jay to give me a lift home.

I tell him about the Sweetheart Ball situation, and he says, "You know you did the right thing, bro."

"I did?"

"Sure. You gotta let them go if you want to hold on to them and all that shit."

"*Errr!*" I growl.

"Down boy," he says.

I hit the sack around ten, wide-awake, a lot on my mind. I think I'll never get to sleep, but the next thing I know Dad is shaking me awake. What? My alarm didn't go off? I'm late for my flight? I press the light button on my watch. 3:46. Then I hear it: thrashing sounds and groans coming from down the hall.

"Another attack," says Dad. "I've never seen her this bad."

I'm on my feet, sprinting down the hall, Dad following. I reach my parents' room in time to see Mom double over, reel off the bed, and lie still.

I pounce on my knees at her side, press my hand against her jugular. Her skin feels both clammy and fiery, her pulse racing beneath it. "She's passed out," I say.

"I'm calling nine-one-one for an ambulance," says Dad.

"No. Call St. Joseph's. Tell them we're on our way. We can get her to the ER sooner than an ambulance can arrive at our door."

"We can't get her into the car. Let the medics handle it."

Medics! My dad knows way more than the EMTs riding ambulances. I leap to my feet. "I'll go get one of the camping cots. We can use it as a stretcher." I stop off at my room to slip on jeans, flip-flops, and a jacket before bounding down the stairs. In the kitchen I grab Dad's Toyota RAV4 keys off the rack, and in the garage I hit the automatic door opener, fold the backseat down in the car, and swing open the hatch door. In less than a minute I'm climbing the stairs again with the folded cot under my arm. This can't be happening! Not on the morning I'm supposed to fly to California.

In my parents' room, Dad is pulling a sweatshirt over his head. I snap open the cot, but not the collapsed legs, and lay it flat next to Mom.

"I don't know about this," he says.

"Get her legs." I lift Mom's shoulders while Dad hoists her hips. We set her on the cot and arrange a blanket over her.

"Let's switch places," I say. "I'll go first, walking backward."

It's a little tricky taking the stairs and keeping Mom level at the same time. She slides toward me, and at one point the cot tilts to the right and we have to pause to balance her weight again. In the living room, we take her out the front door, around the walk, and slide her cot into the rear of the waiting SUV.

"What about a seat belt?" asks Dad.

"I'll be careful." I head for the driver's seat and Dad gets in the passenger's side. Once we're on the road, he calls the hospital to tell them we're coming and Mom may need immediate attention. He dials nine-one-one to describe our vehicle and explain we are going over the speed limit due to an emergency. Finally, he texts Meredith to let her know what's going on. He reaches behind him and strokes Mom's hair as she groans in her unconscious state.

I drive as fast as I can without being reckless. Soon after we merge onto the freeway, a highway patrol glides in ahead of us, his lights flashing, and escorts us to the off-ramp and through red lights to the entrance of St. Joseph's Hospital. At the emergency room door, medics are waiting for us with a gurney, and they transfer Mom onto it. Dad walks alongside her as they wheel her inside while I park the car.

When I return to the building, I find that Mom on her gurney has disappeared through the swinging double doors, and Dad is seated in the waiting room, hunched over a clipboard with a pile of paperwork to fill out. I sink wearily into a chair next to him. "Have you found out anything?"

He looks at me, his eyes bleary, his hair standing on end. "Dr. Malton suspects a ruptured appendix."

"You know this doctor?"

"Just met him. New hiree. A young guy, but he comes highly recommended."

"Do you think Mom has appendicitis symptoms?"

"Not really, but it's painful enough for her to pass out. They're going to do an ultrasound and a CAT scan to check for gallstones."

"That will take awhile."

"Uh-huh." His phone rings, and he checks it. "It's Meredith." He answers and begins telling my sister about the morning's events. When he hangs up, he returns to his paperwork. Does he remember I'm supposed to be at the airport in a few hours? I check my watch. 4:37. I can still make it.

In another two hours I'm not so sure.

Glory texts me: "Bye-bye, babe."

I reply: "In ER for Mom. Bad attack."

"Sorry! Gallbladder?"

"Running tests."

Another ten minutes pass before Glory responds by text: "Request a HIDA."

Dad has dozed off. I nudge him awake with my elbow. "What's a HIDA?"

"Hmm . . . type of scan."

I look up the acronym on my phone: "hepatobiliary iminodiacetic acid." Great. That's means absolutely nothing to me. "Glory texted me that Mom should have one done."

"I'm sure Dr. Malton will do whatever is necessary."

At the mention of his name, the doctor bursts through the swinging door, a bounce to his step. He's a wiry white guy about my height, with a single diamond stud earring and a soul patch. Dad and I rise from our chairs as he greets us with a clap of his hands and self-assured grin. "Good news first or bad?"

I wonder how there can be anything bad to say accompanied by that smirk on his face, but Dad says, "Good."

"CAT scan was normal. No gallstones. Appendix is healthy, too."

"So what's wrong with her?" I ask.

"Ah, that's the bad news. Couldn't find a thing. Say, we haven't met. Are you Evan?" We shake hands. His forearm is tattooed with the medical symbol, a staff entwined by two snakes and topped with wings. "Connie did mention that she's stressed out about you going on some big bike tour."

"She can talk?" asks Dad.

"Oh, yeah. She's resting comfortably now. I'm going to keep her for a twenty-four-hour observation, just as a precaution. You can see her as soon as she's admitted to the hospital."

"Good," says Dad. "Thank you very much, doctor." He claps me on the back. "We'll have just enough time for you to say good-bye to Mom before I run you to the airport."

"Stress doesn't usually cause someone to pass out," I say to Dr. Malton. "We'd like more tests, a HIDA scan to start."

Dr. Malton crosses his forearms, his tattoo on top, and tilts his chin. "Ah, yes. Connie mentioned you wanted to be a doctor. And what might a HIDA scan do, Dr. Evan?"

I haven't a clue. I wish I had time to research it before this arrogant dick approached us. "Uh . . . find out what's wrong with my mom?"

"I see," he says, nodding. "Well, you aren't a doctor yet, are you?" He looks at Dad. "I don't think there's any call for a HIDA, but as administrator of our very own ICU, Connie is my favorite patient. I'll provide her with all the care she needs."

"I know you will, doctor." Dad gently tugs at the crook of my arm. "Come on, Ren. By the time we walk over to admissions, they'll probably have Mom's room number for us."

Dad leads me through a long corridor to outside doors. We're at the crosswalk between buildings waiting at a red light when Glory texts: "WHAT'S HAPPENING?"

"CAT SHOWS NOTHING. IN FOR 24 HR OB."

"HIDA?"

"No."

The light changes to green, and Dad starts to cross just as Glory texts me again: "Get the HIDA."

I stare at Glory's message a few seconds, then look up at Dad, who is strolling along with his hands in his pockets and whistling a tune. If young Dr. Malton can't diagnose Mom, then there's a whole staff of doctors that can. Certainly her own hospital won't let her die on us. I'll just ignore Glory's text, visit with Mom a bit, and catch my flight.

But something about this feels totally wrong. "Dad! Wait!" I shout, and dash after him.

I convince him to return to the emergency room to request the HIDA scan. We take our seats in the waiting room again as a clerk behind a glass window makes some phone calls. It takes awhile. Seven thirty rolls around, the time I'm supposed to be at the airport. How close can I cut it? Sky Harbor is a big place. You don't just show up for a flight ten minutes before take off.

Finally the clerk gets off the phone. Instead of calling Dad to the window, she comes out a side door and moves toward us, hopefully with some answers. Out of my peripheral vision, I see a teen girl balancing a laptop on one forearm and manipulating its keys with the other as she bursts through the outside doors. It's Glory, dressed in pajama pants and a hoodie and wearing glasses instead of contacts.

"Glory?" I run up to her and grab two handfuls of wild hair, sparkly with raindrops. "Whoa, I love what you've done with your hair!"

She rolls her eyes. "Obviously nothing!" She steps around me and greets my dad. "Hi, Mr. Boroughs, did you get the HIDA ordered?"

The clerks replies for him. "I'm sorry. Your insurance won't authorize it unless the doctor of record requests it."

"Thank you," replies Dad, and the woman walks away.

"God's sake, get another doctor of record," says Glory. "Look at this." She tilts her laptop so Dad can get a better view of the screen. "HIDA imaging tracks the flow of bile from the liver to the small intestine. It can detect any blockage." Glory continues her spiel, moving through several sites she has bookmarked.

After a few minutes Dad touches her shoulder, interrupting her. "Thanks for checking into this, Glory. I'll definitely mention it to Dr. Malton. In the meantime, let's go over and see Connie, and then I've got to run our TOC rider over to the airport. Excuse me, I'm going to visit the men's room first."

As he rounds the corner Glory snaps her computer shut and stashes it in her bag. She leans into me, muttering, "He's going to *mention* it?"

"Dad's been acting weird. It's like as long as we don't find anything seriously wrong with Mom, she's just fine."

"You're no better. You're hopping a plane at a time like this?"

"Damn it, Glory. Don't guilt-trip me. Whatever happens to Mom will happen whether I'm here or not."

She shakes her head. "What happens to your mom depends on the care she gets. If there's blockage, the gallbladder could rupture, and the abdominal cavity filling with bacteria is death. Your mom could have a time bomb in her gut. Are you going to do something about it, Evan?"

"Shit!" I drop my face in my hands and stagger around in little circles, trying to think straight. "What if the HIDA scan doesn't show anything?"

"Then there's the liver to explore. The small intestine, the stomach, the pancreas."

"Like it could be pancreatic cancer? No one survives that!" I blot my eyes with the ends of my fists. Soon I feel Glory's smooth, firm fingers wrap around my wrists. She pulls my hands down and moves her face inches from me. "It's her gallbladder. You've seen her attacks, babe. Notice how she moves her hands to her back, clear to her shoulder blades? People don't act like that with pancreatic cancer. I've got a strong hunch it's acute cholecystitis."

I exhale a deep, shuddering sigh. "All right. I'll call Mike and tell him I'm not coming today. I can reschedule my flight for tomorrow. Probably I can get away then."

Glory looks doubtful. "Maybe your riding the Tour of California just isn't meant to be. Everything happens for a reason."

"You don't believe that crap."

"I'm trying to help."

"You are helping." I take her into my arms.

Dad strides up to us. "Let's hustle. You don't want to miss your flight, Ren."

"I'm not going."

I dread calling Mike Townsend, but when I explain my situation, he's understanding, even sympathetic. Today I'll be missing time trial practice, where I was supposed to be fitted on my time trial bike and practice riding the actual course in downtown Sacramento. It's short, technical, and fast, with lots of tight corners, railroad tracks, and other hazards. It will be murder racing it as unfamiliar territory.

"It's not that important," says Mike. "Remember your focus is Stage Three. Wish your mother well from the team, and we'll see you tomorrow."

It's easy to get another "doctor of record." Malton is replaced by Dr. Myers, the gastroenterologist Mom was scheduled to see next Tuesday. The first thing he does is order a HIDA scan, so I don't know if Glory's insistence and my missing my flight made any difference in the outcome.

In the afternoon during the HIDA scan, Mom is on the examining table nearly two hours, and not a drop of bile seeps into her gallbladder the entire time. Dr. Myers books her for surgery first thing the next morning to remove her gallbladder, a cholecystectomy. I miss my flight again, so I can sit out the operation in the waiting room with Dad and Meredith, who has driven home from Santa Barbara. It turns out that Mom had an enlarged gallbladder caused by an infection that left some areas of it blackened with gangrene. If it had burst, it could have killed her.

Glory dutifully offers to cancel her dance plans, since I'm in town after all Saturday night, but I encourage her to go on, have fun. Dad, Meredith, and I are hanging out in Mom's hospital room, sipping orange juice, when Glory sends me her photo.

"Whoa, that dress is hot," says Meredith, peering over my shoulder. "You let her out with another guy looking like that? You're crazy."

I just grind my teeth.

I board a flight to Sacramento Sunday morning, five hours before the race start. Peering out the window, watching Phoenix, dotted with turquoise swimming pools, fall away, I feel disoriented, apprehensive, exhausted. Yet when I lean back and take a few deep breaths, a warm satisfaction washes over me. Mom is doing fine and gets to live pain free from now on. I saw to it with Glory's help.

Now that that's taken care of, I'm good to go.

Part Two

The Race

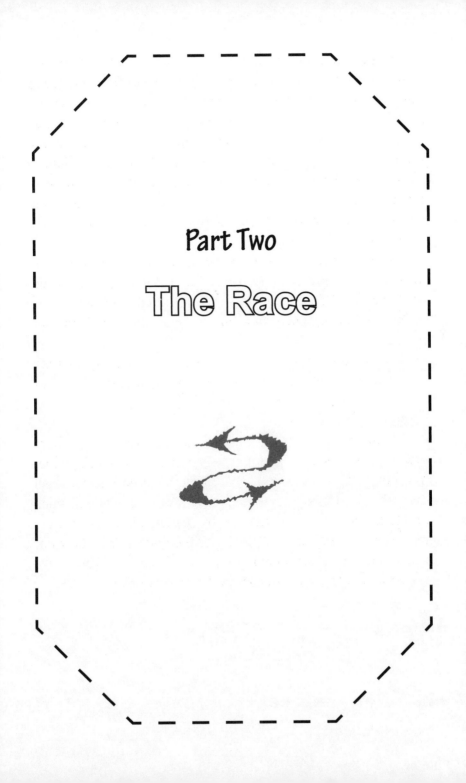

Chapter Eight

Stage 1: Sacramento Time Trial, 12 Miles

The waiting crowd hollers and hoots as I step out of the Image Craft–Icon "bus," actually a luxury motor home. I'm standing in a space three yards wide and running the length of the bus, a sort of pen with portable, waist-high fencing used to keep the spectators from pressing too close. The cheers immediately die down as the fans realize it's just me, a lowly domestique, and not Dashiell Shipley. Cameras flash, aimed not at me but our time trial bikes, worth over ten grand each, which one of our mechanics, Pablo Santos, is lining up against the bus.

With less than an hour before the noon start, thousands of people are gathered behind the bright yellow Tour of California barriers along the Sacramento Capitol Mall. The sun is trying to come out above the white dome of the capitol building. It rained last night, but the streets are dry enough for fans to chalk messages to the riders, many of them love letters to Dash.

Time trials give people a chance to see their favorite riders up close and personal. In a road race the tightly packed peloton whirls by in a matter of seconds. In time trials the riders are ranked slowest to fastest, and launched out of the start house at one-minute intervals. A time trial is short, but it's a grueling race, one man against the clock. No drafting allowed.

Since I'm one of the least experienced riders, I'm the fifth man up, while Dash Shipley will be fourth from the last. Following him will be Fernando Iglesias of Banco de Madrid, winner of the *Vuelta a España*; Dash's ex-teammate and nemesis Klaus Grunwald of Kronen, the World Time Trial Champion; and Temir Laptev of Taraz, last year's winner of the Tour of California. With over two hours between my start and the leaders, riding conditions will change radically. Lucky me, I get the good weather; the favorites won't. More rain is predicted in the afternoon, with increasing winds.

The crowd cheers as Dash emerges from our bus. He smiles and waves, but does not immediately step forward to the pens and programs extended over the fence. "Trade ya start positions," he says to me.

"I would if I could."

"I know. You're going to be a big help to me. How do you feel?"

"Not ready," I admit. "I didn't get to try my time trial bike or ride the course."

Rainier Laurent approaches us. He looks me up and down and says, "Oh, are you still on this team? There's more to it than just showing up for the race."

He talks like he isn't aware of my situation, even though

I know Mike has kept the team informed. I start explaining, "My mom had emergency surgery, and I had to make sure—"

His impatient fingers flutter in the air. It's a gesture I've noticed that Rainier commonly uses, as if whoever is talking is wasting his time. "I've heard the whole story. I've also heard your mother isn't in favor of you riding the TOC. Interesting that she would develop such medical problems on the day you were scheduled to depart." He struts off.

I turn to Dash and blurt, "She could've died!"

He touches my shoulder. "You did the right thing, Evan. How much do you think all this meant to me when I discovered Logan was seriously ill? Lance Armstrong said it best when he was battling cancer. 'It's not about the bike.' Life holds greater value." He pats his side. "People said if I donated a kidney to Logan, it would put an end to my career, but they were wrong. My son is alive and here I am."

Dash is sincere, but his little spiel sounds canned. Still, he has worked his magic. I feel a lot better just moments after Rainier made me feel like shit. I lean in to him to disclose my greatest fear: "What if I'm the slowest today?"

"What of it?" he says, laughing. "But you won't be. Not in these conditions."

I stare down the street at the TV cameramen setting up their equipment on the first sharp turn. There's sure to be some spills there, especially on wet pavement. This is where the biggest crowd gathers. I shudder, imagining them and millions of TV viewers around the world watching me slide through the corner on my face.

"Dash! Dash! Over here!"

Boisterous teenage girls push one another as they lean farther over the fence. Dash steps forward to sign their programs and flirt with them. As I walk down the line of bikes looking for mine I feel a tap on my shoulder.

It's one of the girls. "Are you somebody?"

"Nope."

She glances over at Dash and then back at me, dressed exactly like him. Our team jersey is blue with white swirling lines. The company logo is front center, with the words IMAGE and CRAFT in white written above and below a jutting red line, and under that is the word ICON, the gold *I* within a black disk. The front and back panels of our shorts are also red, with blue side panels.

The girl cocks her hip and looks me over. "You're like one of Dash's teammates, aren't you?" She thrusts a program and a Sharpie into my hands. "Here. Sign."

This is an occasion: my first autograph request. The program is the Sacramento version; each host city has its own. I flip through it to find a photo of Image Craft–Icon riding in tight formation, with only the stoic faces of Dash, Bernard, Salvatore Netti, and Charles Larocque visible. I begin to sign what I think might be my right knee when the girl yanks her program away and thrusts it in front of Dash, causing me to scrawl a black streak down the page.

Rainier approaches me again and says, "Why are you standing around? You should be warming up!"

I jog around the bus to where Pablo set my time trial bike on a trainer, a device with a roller that attaches to the rear wheel and transforms a regular bike into a stationary one. I don't own one because I don't like them. If I'm going to ride, I want to be going some place. I mount the bike and get the cranks spinning while Pablo studies my positioning with a critical eye. He stops me several times to make minor adjustments to the seat post, the saddle, and the bars. On the trainer there's no sense of balance, handling, or steering. I'm eager to try the bike out on the road, but there's no chance this close to the start. My warmup should take at least forty minutes.

I frequently check my watch, keeping close track of the time. The biggest, dumbest mistake a rider can make in a time trial is missing his start time.

Mike Townsend bounds out of the bus, yelling, "Evan, what are you doing here? You're supposed to be in the start house right now!"

I wonder what's the hurry. "There's four guys ahead of me."

"Not anymore. Some riders have canceled last minute, and the roster has been adjusted. You're up first, in seven minutes."

"I'm first? Oh, shit!" I jump off the bike and shed my leggings while Pablo disengages my bike from the trainer. I open the fence to leave.

"Your helmet!" Mike calls.

"Your radio!" shouts Pablo.

I shift my weight from one foot to the other as Pablo fits my two-way radio earpiece in place so Mike and Rainier can communicate with me during the race. I slap on my time-trialing helmet, which is teardrop shaped, so that the flow of air rides over my head and down my back.

I dash down the mall and climb the back steps of the start house, a tiny structure three feet off the ground with a ramp attached to the front. Minutes before my start, I mount my bike. The starter's assistant straddles my rear wheel and holds me upright while I clip into both pedals. I'm shaking so bad, it takes me several tries to snap my right cleat into place.

Mike is speaking into my radio. "Steady now, Evan. Deep breaths."

The starter says, "Twenty seconds. Ten." He holds four fingers in front of me, then three, two, one. "Go!"

I rise out of the saddle, stomp on the right pedal, then the left, trying to grind into motion a gear larger than I normally use. I soar down the ramp, and my front wheel hits the street with a thump. A waiting motorcycle roars out ahead of me, and Mike and Rainier follow me in the team car, heading toward Tower Bridge.

Blaring over the PA, the announcer says, "Colin Teague of Team Mobile Electric, the first of one hundred twenty-eight riders, has launched the Tour of California!"

Over the thunderous cheers of the crowd, his correction is barely audible. "Sorry, folks. There's been a change of program. This is . . . Who is this? This is Evan Boroughs of Image Craft–Icon."

Nothing feels right. The fit of the time trial bike is so tight that my knees nearly hit my elbows as I'm tucked in against the wind, my shoulders pressed forward. I bet I could ride better on my own road bike, left at home. I can't even ride it on the road because, like every pro team, ours is licensed with a specific bike manufacturer. A time trial bike is way different from a road bike. It's built to be aerodynamic, light, stiff, and strong. It's not built for comfort, since time trials are short.

I'm extended over the front of my bike, stretched out on aerobars. They position me low and flat for less wind resistance, but I'm not used to them. I have to hold up my upper body with my forearms and steer with them at the same time, making me feel rocky. The rear wheel is a solid disc, which makes a weird flapping sound. I could do better if only I'd had a chance to try the bike ahead of time.

"Evan, you don't have to be this conservative," says Rainier. "Take it up a notch."

I realize I've been so cautious, I'm not even breathing hard. What if the guy who starts a minute behind me catches me? How humiliating! I glance behind me, and my forearms naturally follow, causing my front wheel to lurch to the left. I straighten out just in time to avoid a spill. According to my power meter, I'm producing 315 watts of energy. I pour on the pressure until I'm gasping for air. My speedometer hits 26 mph, then 29. I'm flying at 32 mph, a strong tailwind pushing me on.

"Slow down, Evan! You're not going to make the turn at that speed," warns Rainier.

With my head down I didn't realize I was so close to the first corner. I brake and skid gracelessly into Old Town, fans crowding the wooden sidewalks. Bouncing along, I feel the jarring cobbles in my bones and teeth. I can't gain much speed before the next turn, and I know I've lost a chunk of time. J Street is smooth asphalt, but now I'm battling a crosswind that comes at me diagonally in powerful gusts, pushing me off course. I'm struggling to churn the pedals, thighs burning, breath coming in raspy gasps as I helplessly watch my speed decrease.

"Keep your head straight!" says Rainier.

"I am!"

"No, it's cocked. Straight on, Evan."

I turn my head slightly and feel the difference, the wind funneling over the top of the helmet. "Is my minute man gaining?" I ask breathlessly.

"You never mind what's behind you. Pay attention to what's ahead."

Finally, mercifully, I'm veering into the turnaround, the circular drive of Sacramento State University. On the return trip I've got a tailwind. The course is flat and fast, the bike is sleek and light, and at last I'm having fun.

I pass riders going the opposite direction, their lead-out motorcycles in front and their team cars behind them. I take the left turn onto Nineteenth Street like a wimp but lay the bike down through the right turn onto L Street. The capitol grounds are in sight now, and my ride is ending. I try to rise out of the saddle to sprint, but my legs are empty. I cross the finish line at Tenth Street completely spent.

I made it! Mike is shouting, "Atta boy! Atta boy!" into my radio, while one of our *soigneurs*, Max Hines, is lifting me off the saddle. Mike steers the team car around to the start house to get ready to follow Dedrick Pieters on his ride.

Our mechanic, George Winslow, takes possession of my bike and wheels it away, not letting it out of his sight. At the 2009 Tour of California, right here in Sacramento, Team Astana's trailer was broken into at night, and Lance Armstrong's time trial bike was stolen. Perhaps the thief had trouble fencing that one-of-a-kind flying machine because it was later recovered, leaning against a tree. George took no chances and bedded down with our bikes in the trailer last night as if they were Kentucky Derby thoroughbreds.

Max hands me his own concoction of a recovery drink, wraps me in a warm-up jacket, and helps me into leggings. All I've got to do now is enjoy the rest of the day watching the other riders come in.

The wind picks up steadily, and about an hour later it begins to rain. The road gets slick, and several riders go down on the turns. While I feel sorry for them, I can't help but feel glad this nasty weather is going to make me look better.

From beneath the awning of our bus, I cheer as wildly as any fan when the announcer states, "Dashiell Shipley of Image Craft–Icon has just rocketed out of the start house."

Finally, it's just the big guns, Dash, Fernando Iglesias, Klaus Grunwald, and Temir Laptev left on the course. When the final results are in, it's not World Time Trialing Champion Klaus Grunwald who wins, but Fernando Iglesias. Klaus is second, three seconds down, and Temir is third, seven seconds down. I'm shocked to see that even Bernard beat Dash by two seconds, coming in fourth, eight seconds down.

I think Dash must be disappointed, but while our team watches the podium ceremony he says, "I'm just where I want to be. No use attracting needless attention this early in the race."

Fernando, Klaus, and Temir mount the three staggered blocks for first, second, and third place. The mayor shakes Fernando's hand, and the race leader's yellow jersey is slipped over his arms. The two podium girls kiss his cheeks simultaneously.

"How'd you do?" Dash asks me.

"Eighty-eighth. A two-minute twenty-one-second gap."

"Hey, that's not bad," says Dash, knocking my fist with his.

"Weather helped."

"When the gods of cycling smile upon you, be happy."

Happy? I'm ecstatic. I call my dad, who says he and Mom were able to watch the race on the TV in her hospital room. He congratulates me on my ride and says Mom is already sitting up, complaining she's hungry.

I'm dying to talk to Glory, but even when we get settled into our hotel in nearby Davis, I have to wait and wait for a private moment. My teammates and I eat dinner together, have our team meeting, and take turns getting massages. As for roommates, we are paired off the same every night: Dash and Bernard, Salvatore Netti and Charles Larocque, Joris and Dedrick Pieters, and I'm stuck with Armand Fitzroy, the French guy Rainier's friend recommended. It would have made more sense if Charles roomed with Armand because Charles, being from Quebec, speaks both French and English.

Armand and I have not hit it off. He's this arrogant little man with a pointy red beard, and he prances around with his toes turned out like a ballet dancer. He thinks it's a personal affront that I don't speak French, and when I tried Spanish he was insulted even more. It's ridiculous because his English is good, but so far I've only heard him use it to criticize America and Americans.

Finally, around nine, Armand leaves the room, and I get a chance to call Glory. "Did you see me?" I blurt as soon as she answers.

"Yeah! But we didn't realize it was you at first. You guys look pretty much alike in your helmets and glasses, and the announcer called you by some other guy's name."

"I wasn't supposed to be first. There was some confusion at the start. I was shaking so bad, I could hardly get my foot in the pedal."

"But you did it! You started off the whole freaking Tour of California!"

"Yeah. How awesome is that? How'd I look?"

"Uh . . . good."

"That's not what you were going say. Out with it, sweet. I can take it."

"Well, you didn't exactly get a chance to practice on that special bike, right?" There's a pause. "You looked a little wobbly, babe."

"Aw, hell!"

"But you didn't crash," she says quickly. "Not like some of those other dudes."

"Uh-huh. It was because I took the corners like a grandma."

Her giggle is ripply. "Good tactic!"

Chapter Nine

Stage 2: Davis to Santa Rosa, 110 Miles

Meredith got accepted to college in Davis, but she snubbed it as a "farm town," preferring UC Santa Barbara, known for its beaches and wild parties. If I got to go to college in California, I'd definitely choose this place. Davis is a cycling town. It's got a comfortable feel, relaxed and friendly. I could get a lot of studying and riding done here.

Again the bright yellow Tour of California barricades line the streets. Some of the spectators show up on their bikes despite the drizzle. Others hold red, heart-shaped helium balloons for Valentine's Day. Back at the hotel, I try calling Glory, but her phone is turned off.

At the start, we take turns mounting the stage and ceremoniously signing in as contestants of the race. Signing-in is required each day. I don't know what happens to the star-studded sign-in sheets, but they would go for a bundle on eBay. The 128 riders begin to assemble at the line, waiting for the eleven-o'clock start. Nearly all of us are wearing rain jackets, a new concept in bike racing, same as helmets. Up until recent years riders only wore short-sleeved jerseys, shorts, and tiny cycling caps no matter what the racing conditions were.

I know it's going to be a tough ride today. Much of the 110 miles will be fast and flat, with two sprints, but there are also four King of the Mountains designations, one close to the beginning and three toward the end.

My Image Craft–Icon teammates and I are at the head of the peloton, clustered around Dash. When Fernando Iglesias shows up wearing the yellow jersey, he rolls in to my left. Lucky me, I'm positioned between two of the greatest cyclists in the world. Fernando waves to the cheering crowd, but his smile quickly fades and his face tenses. He's worried about something, maybe holding on to the yellow jersey. He looks up at the sky and blinks out the raindrops falling in his eyes.

"*Llueve a cántaros*," I comment, which pretty much means it's raining buckets.

He smiles at being addressed in his native language. "They say the sun always shines in California," he replies in Spanish, his Castilian accent much different from the American Spanish I'm used to hearing.

"*Eso es mentira*," I say. That's a lie.

He grins, raising his chin. A teammate taps him on the shoulder and speaks at length in rapid Castilian Spanish.

Dash elbows me and nods toward Fernando. "Don't let your new friend out of your sight."

Now I have two jobs: sit in the pack *and* keep an eye on the yellow jersey. I don't know if both are possible simultaneously.

The horn blares for the start, and we roll through a three-mile neutral zone. After that, the pace revs up to a fast, but not searing, speed. Every direction I look, it's as flat as a pancake. I expect nothing will happen until we get to the hills, but at mile eight a BISSELL rider sprints ahead on a breakaway. Is he crazy? A solo break over one hundred miles, alone in the wind and the rain?

The peloton lets him go. Within the next two minutes the gap opens to 15 seconds, 30, a minute. Two Rabobank riders chase after the leader. Oftentimes riders who have little chance of winning a whole race will breakaway for a stage win. An early break like this is hardly ever successful, but some guys think it's worth a try. The TV cameras are always focused on a breakaway, and sponsors love their company names in the spotlight.

At mile 13, we pass into the town of Winters. The locals line the streets to cheer us on, but they will not have much of a show. There's no need for the peloton to contest the sprint, since the three men in the breakaway have already cleaned up the sprint points. Leaving Winters, our own sprinter, Charles, punctures, and after our team car supplies him with a wheel change Joris and Dedrick fall back with him to pace him back to the peloton.

By mile 20 the breakaway has gained a 3-minute lead. I glance over at Dash, but he doesn't look a bit concerned, keeping his eyes peeled on Armand's rear wheel. The other three race leaders—Fernando, Temir, and Klaus—are also tucked away in the peloton behind their domestiques, in no hurry to chase.

We enter Napa County. All around us are green hills, yellow mustard, and rows and rows of grape vines. It would be beautiful if it weren't for the pouring rain. At last we begin the first climb, a Category 4, up Monticello Dam. It's a short hill with an elevation gain of a thousand feet, but at last it's something to do. I'm relieved to rise out of the saddle and generate some body heat. The riders who pushed the pace on the flat are not as eager on the climb. I find myself surging off the front without trying.

"Evan, take it easy," says Dash. "You'll get your chance to pound up the mountains tomorrow."

I ease up, but it's disappointing. The peloton is climbing at a slower pace than I would like, and it throws off my rhythm. Sal is eager to get moving, too, and when he rolls off the front, Dash doesn't call him back. If he can catch the breakaway, he'll earn King of the Mountains points, then be able to block its progress. Soon Mike announces over our radios that two of the men in the breakaway are fading, and Sal does manage to overtake them to come in second in KOM points.

We descend along Lake Berryessa in thick mist. Close to mile forty, I'm getting hungry. I look down the road in search of the feed zone. There Max will have our "hand ups," energy bars, gel packs, and drinks packed in a musette, a cotton bag with a long strap that fits over the shoulder and diagonally crosses the body. After claiming our musettes, we will grab the food out of the bag, stuff it into our mouths and jersey pockets, then throw the bag at the side of the road.

Except that when we enter the feed zone, Max isn't there. The weather and road conditions have caused a delay for a number of the teams' *soigneurs* to be in place in time to feed. Lucky for some teams; not lucky for us. There's groans and curses from the riders who don't get supplies. I turn my head and happen to notice that a blue jersey, not yellow, is beside me. I search all around for Fernando, thinking the confusion at the feed zone has caused the riders to shuffle in the peloton.

No sign of the yellow jersey anywhere.

"Fernando! He's gone!" I exclaim to Dash.

"Where to?"

"I don't know! He was here a minute ago."

"We'd certainly notice if he jumped off the front." He jerks his head backward, gesturing to the rear of the peloton. "There's only one other direction. Drop back, Evan. Maybe he's planning something with his teammates out of earshot."

I do what I'm told, but it worries me. If I let go of my position now, I'll have to fight my way to the front again. I move to the left and slow my pedaling, allowing the riders to swish past me. In the last third of the peloton, I spot Fernando.

He's not pedaling. He veers toward the shoulder, unclips his feet, and straddles his bike.

I slowly coast by him. "*¿Fernando, qué pasa?*"

"*Estoy enfermo.*" He is shivering, hugging himself in shaking arms, sweat dripping from his face.

"*¡Qué lastimá!*" I don't wait to watch him slip into his team car and withdraw from the race, but that's what happens.

I'm stunned. Fernando Iglesias, the wearer of the yellow jersey, one of the three greatest threats to Dash's win, is gone, wiped out due to illness in Stage 2! I should be elated, but somehow I'm disappointed. He was such a nice guy, so friendly to me. Already I had imagined having more chats with him.

Working my way toward the front, I notice cyclists on the side of the road due to "mechanicals." The rough road has caused many flats, but there's other problems, too. Team cars stop, and mechanics jump out to assist the riders.

From my radio I hear Rainier's command. "Evan, pull over." I look around to see our team car driving slowly at the side of the road. I glide up to it and hook my elbow over the rear open window of the moving car. I shed my rain jacket, which feels like soggy dead weight.

Mike explains quickly. "You're going to have to feed the guys up front."

Dash doesn't want me to feed today because of the extra energy it takes, but I don't argue. Nobody ever expected our supplies wouldn't get to the feed zone on time, nor that Joris and Dedrick would have to drop back to tow Charles to the peloton, nor that Sal would decide to attack on his own. That's leaves Dash pretty shorthanded, with just Armand and Bernard taking pulls when we're all supposed to be working for him.

Rainier hands me three extra water bottles, which I stash in the inside pockets of my domestique jersey, and three bulging musettes, which I drape across my body. When I push away from the car, the added weight knocks me off-balance. My bike wavers as I struggle for control.

Up ahead there's a loud bang, a scraping of metal, and shouts of surprise and anger. A tire exploded, the rider slowed, and another rider plowed into him, causing a pileup of about twenty riders. Stuck behind the crash, I watch the peloton roll out of sight. Now how am I going to get supplies to my teammates?

Soon after I pick my way through the fallen riders, I hear from behind me, "Evan! Jump on!"

I turn to see Joris, Dedrick, and Charles rocketing toward me as part of a five-man paceline. As it snakes by me I leap out of the saddle to catch the rear position. One of my stowed water bottles launches out of my jersey and bombs my front spokes. The wheel hops and skids, and I think I'm going down, but somehow I manage to keep the bike upright.

The paceline streaks up the road without me. I'm dropped off the back. A loser. If only I had thought to hand my teammates some of the heavy supplies. I'm puffing and exhausted. How can I do Dash any good tomorrow? I can't even stay with the peloton today.

I fall into an off-the-back group of a dozen or so riders, called the *gruppetto*, Italian for "small group." It's humiliating to be there because it usually consists of sprinters and other riders who are not strong enough to keep up on the climbs, and I'm supposed to be a climbing specialist.

Through my radio Rainier orders me, "Drop your load, Evan. I fed the team myself."

More humiliation. I'm not even working out as water boy.

"You hear me?"

"Yeah."

"Respond then. Keep some food for yourself and eat."

Another mistake. I'm hauling around a whole food market, and I haven't taken a bite. I can't eat. My stomach is in knots. I stuff some of the energy gels and bars in my jersey pockets, thinking I'll feel better later.

"Evan? Answer!"

"Yeah?"

"Eat."

"Okay!" I tear a foil gel open with my teeth and squeeze its contents into my mouth. My eyes water and I cough. I'm choking on viscous fudge syrup, but I swallow hard, force it down, and chase it with water.

"Don't lose heart, Evan," says Rainier almost sympathetically.

"I'm not," I mutter.

"Speak up!"

"I'm not! I'm *fine*!"

Through my earpiece I hear laughter from both Mike and Rainier. If they think it's so damn funny, let them get out of a warm car and try slogging through the chilling rain—but I know both of them have. Nearly all team managers and *directeur sportifs* are retired riders.

I toss my two empty water bottles out of their cages onto the roadside and replace them with full ones out of my jersey.

I lift one of the musettes over my head and am about to drop it when a rider hopefully asks, "Anything left?"

"Sure," I say. "Lots."

I pass the musettes throughout the whole group. There's cheers and laughter. Party in the *gruppetto*, sponsored by Image Craft–Icon. I doubt Mike would like me feeding other teams, but whatever. These guys aren't going to take anything away from Dash.

We turn left and begin the ascent up Howell Mountain Road. It's a steep, Category 2, 1,800-foot climb, rising through forests. It feels great to stretch my legs, and within the first mile I leave the *gruppetto* behind. I stuff down an energy bar and drink what I can. The road twists and turns, so that it is hard to see far ahead, but I hear cheers from above, which tells me the peloton is not far. If only this climb were a few miles longer, I could catch it.

Toward the summit, the fans get louder and press farther into the road. It seems like I'm riding though a tunnel made of people. Some guys jump into the road to take pictures, moving out of the way in the nick of time. One Statue-of-Liberty guy runs directly ahead of me, so I have to swerve to miss his torch.

"Goooooooooooo, Evaaaaaaaaaaaan!" someone screams in my ear. I turn my head to see a guy dressed in a superhero's outfit: blue tights, red cape, and a gigantic Afro. "E-van, E-van, can't you do better than that?"

This guy is so annoying, I want to smack him. How does he know who I am? Of course, anyone with a program can look up my number, 123, and find my name.

I crest the mountain, and a spectator hands me a section of newspaper, which I tuck inside my soaking jersey for warmth on the descent. I plunge into the foggy abyss, my wheels shooting up spray from the slippery, wet roads. What if I go one way and the road goes another? Headlines reporting my death loom in my mind. I pump the brakes more than I need to. When I'm on flatter ground, I'm farther behind than I was at the summit.

Rainier informs me that the breakaway is now eight minutes in the lead. It's often surprising how wide of a gap the peloton allows before the riders begin to organize a chase, but it's all about strategy. A bike race is like a rolling chess match: the right moves have to be made at the right time. The best way to catch a breakaway is to time it so close to the finish that another break has no chance to form. Right now the only dangerous member of the four-man breakaway is our own teammate Salvatore Netti. How can this be? It makes no sense to me, but then it's Rainier's job to command Dash's army, not mine.

At mile 82, the 1,000-foot, Category 3 Oakville Grade begins. I ride about two miles up and two miles down, which brings me to the base of the final climb of the day, the 1,800-foot, Category 2 Trinity Grade.

Over my radio I hear the news of a twelve-man chase group forming, including Dash, Bernard, Temir Laptev and his Taraz teammates, Klaus Grunwald and his Kronen teammates, and anyone else who can hang on. The chase group steadily gobbles up the breakaway's lead, which shrinks down to 7:20 at mile 88 and 4:32 at the summit of Trinity Grade. By mile 104 the breakaway splinters apart. At mile 108 the three dazed and exhausted riders who broke away nearly a hundred miles ago are caught by the chase group and passed.

Only Sal is out in front. He makes a two-mile solo run and crosses the finish line 1:06 ahead of the chase group. Every rider in the chase group receives the same time, and when the peloton rolls in 32 seconds later, all of those riders get the same time, too. This is to avoid bunch sprints once the winner of a stage is decided, which prevents massive crashes.

When I roll over the finish line another two minutes or so later, I'm both devastated and exhilarated. On the one hand, I was off the back; on the other, Stage 2 is over, and I finished all 110 grueling miles of it.

It's more like a personal accomplishment, and I feel embarrassed to face my team. Dash strides up to me, slaps me on the back, and says, "You're just the guy I want to see, Evan. Mike said you were bringing me lunch."

I must have a horrified look on my face because Dash's tanned face breaks into his white, Hollywood grin, and I realize he's kidding.

At the podium ceremony Sal is handed a bouquet of flowers and a stuffed California brown bear for winning the stage. The podium girls stand on both sides of him and kiss his cheeks at once. He throws his bouquet into the crowd. Next, he extends his arms and a yellow jersey is placed on him and zipped up the back. It's surprising to see a teammate of mine other than Dash in the yellow jersey. I never even considered it happening.

Sal bows and throws kisses at the audience. He is so loose-jointed, it seems like he has rubber bands for tendons. He's the happiest rider I've ever met, and to make him even happier, he is in love. A story in *VeloNews* said this rich lady from Montana followed him all over Europe last summer as a sort of personal groupie, and at the end of the Tour de France, they became engaged.

The podium ceremony continues. The green sprinter's jersey is presented, and the red King of the Mountain jersey is also awarded to Sal. I look fondly upon the white Best Young Rider jersey, but since I'm nearly six minutes down in the

General Classification, it's far from my grasp. Lastly, the blue Most Courageous Rider jersey is also claimed.

After the awards Dash pumps Sal's hand.

Sal tilts his head, almost apologetically. "I feel good. I go," he explains. He speaks English only in the present tense although he seems to understand it well.

"That's great. You go, Sal!" If Dash is bothered by Sal's taking the lead, he doesn't show it.

As I'm walking with Dash to the team bus a fan yells out, "Hey, Dash, did you fill your kidney with drugs before you gave it to your kid, or is being a doper a recent thing with you?"

Dash stops, looks thoughtfully in the direction of the heckler, then continues to walk on calmly. "You know why people act that way, Evan?"

After a pause I suggest, "Low self-esteem?"

Dash laughs uproariously, as if it's the funniest thing he's ever heard. Clapping my shoulder, he says, "Yeah, that's it. Low self-esteem."

We travel to San Francisco and settle in our hotel near Fisherman's Wharf. I've never been here, and it would be cool to walk the streets and see the sights, but after a team dinner and a massage all I can do is flop onto the bed. Armand has more energy. He dresses in slacks and tucks a little silk scarf into his collar.

"Going out on the town?" I ask him.

He sniffs.

"Whereabouts?"

He sniffs again. Sniffing, I've learned, is the way he answers me. At first I was put off by it, but now I'm so tired, I just laugh. He prances before the full mirror, looking at himself frontways, sideways, and over his shoulder.

"Ass checks out okay, Armand?" I hoot to the ceiling like a crazed hyena.

He pads out of the room, shutting the door soundly.

At last I can call Glory. All day I've been dying to wish her a Happy Valentine's Day. Her phone rings, but she doesn't answer, probably because she's out to dinner with her parents. I hope it's not Alfred. It's Valentine's Day, damn it. Isn't my valentine going to give me a chance to tell her I love her? I hang up without leaving a message. I call my folks, and they put me on speakerphone in Mom's hospital room.

"We thought we saw you in the beginning," says Mom, "but not after that."

"That's because I was off the back!" I explain what happened.

"Don't let it get to you, Ren," says Dad. "It's just a little bad luck."

"What place are you?" asks Mom.

"Seventy-sixth."

"Well, it's not last," she says in a tone that indicates it might as well be.

"And tomorrow is your big day, Ren."

Before I get to comment on that, Mom blurts, "And the next day after that you'll be coming home."

"I told you, Mom, that's not a for-sure thing."

We talk a while longer, then before hanging up, Mom says, "See you Wednesday."

A spot about the race comes on the local news, so I turn up the TV to hear it. The backdrop is soggy downtown Santa Rosa at the finish line.

The newscaster says, "We have race favorite Dashiell Shipley on hand to talk to us. How is your team holding up in this wet weather, Dash?"

"Great so far. As you know, our teammate Sal Netti took the yellow jersey today."

"So you've got stiff competition within your own ranks?"

"A strong team has to have many strong riders."

"I hear the youngest rider in the Tour of California is on your team."

"That's right. Evan Boroughs, an enormous talent. I spotted him at a winter training camp, and I was immediately taken with his climbing skill."

"Do you think he can claim the white jersey?"

"It's a definite possibility."

"Really? An eighteen-year-old can withstand the rigors of an eight-day, seven-hundred-mile stage race?"

Dash looks into the distance, sucks in his breath, cocks his head, and then stares straight into the camera. "I believe Evan can do it."

That's not what he told me. Does he really believe that "enormous talent" stuff, or is that all just talk, too?

I turn off the TV, pull Dante's *Inferno* out of my bag, and try to read. It's tough going, and I keep falling asleep, then waking myself up when the book hits my face. Dante has it wrong: bike racing should also be one ring of hell.

Armand returns with a loaf of bread tucked under his arm and carrying two large, clinking shopping bags. On the counter in the kitchenette, he sets out the bread, a knife, a wedge of cheese, and a thick bar of Ghirardelli's chocolate. A delightful bedtime snack.

From his sport bag he extracts a black leather case that looks something like the ones diabetics carry. Is he diabetic? A doper? I lift myself on my elbows to see if there's a syringe in the case. There are two wineglasses and a corkscrew. For a second I think he might offer me one of the glasses, but no. He removes only one and shuts the case.

He ceremoniously uncorks one of the bottles of wine. He pours a swallow into his glass, swirls it around, sniffs it, swirls it some more, and drains it. Thoughtfully he swishes it around in his mouth like mouthwash and spits it into the sink. He pours the contents of the bottle after it.

"Wow, that's a waste of vino," I say. "No good, huh?"

He ignores me and opens another bottle, takes a taste, and pours it down the drain. I've seen people enjoy wine, but I've never seen anyone enjoy not enjoying wine.

I rest awhile longer, then drag myself down to the dining room for an evening snack of chicken and pasta. Bike racers can never eat as many calories as they burn. When I return to our room, Armand is already in bed asleep. Tiptoeing to my side of the room, I happen to notice a credit card receipt on the floor. I pick it up to set it on his nightstand. I notice the store is San Francisco Wine Cellars and the amount is several hundred dollars. Whoa, expensive Drano.

I'm awakened by the sounds of Armand retching into the toilet. Apparently he didn't pour *all* his wine down the drain. It's still dark. I check my watch: 2:10. I remember I never did get a hold of Glory to wish her a Happy Valentine's Day. Guess I'll finally have to settle for a text, knowing she's asleep and won't see it for several hours.

I write, "HAPPY VD" and am just about to hit the send button when I realize how totally wrong that is. Some things in texts you just can't abbreviate. I edit my message to "HAPPY V DAY," then send.

I flop wearily back on my pillow to the sounds of Armand puking his guts out. My phone vibrates in my hand. It's not a return text but a phone call.

I answer, "Hey."

"Technically, it's not Valentine's Day anymore," she says.

"I'm sorry. I tried calling a few times but—"

"Thanks for the necklace."

"The necklace?" Long, long ago, last Thursday, I gave Glory a little velvet box, and in it was a silver charm of a bicycle on a thin silver chain. I realize now it's all wrong. "It's for you to remember me by."

"I got that. It's working. I'm wearing it right now and not much else."

"Oh, Glory, I miss you!"

"Me, too."

With an agonizing groan, Armand falls into bed.

"What was that?"

"My roommate."

"Oh! What's he like?"

"Hold on." I get up, step into flip-flops, pick up my room key, and go sit in the carpeted hall. "You were asking about Armand. He's about twenty-five, irritable, and snooty."

"Wow, what's his problem?"

"He's French."

"Oh! Can I talk to him sometime? I'd love to practice my French with a native speaker."

"He would only ridicule your accent."

"I'd love a constructive critique. What part of France is he from?"

I don't know why we're going on about Armand. "He won't talk to me, because I don't speak French."

"Hmm. Isn't the Tour de France like the most prestigious bicycle race in the world? Essentially, French is the native tongue of your sport."

"You're taking sides with Armand? Against me?"

She giggles. "I'm just saying consider his point of view. I hope if you ever ride the Tour de France, you will have learned the language by then. It's only common courtesy to your host country."

"I don't think I'm quite ready for the TDF. I'm out of my league here. Do you realize, Glory, today's the big day? What if I blow it?"

"This Shipley guy seems pretty smart. I don't think he would have given you the job if you couldn't handle it. Just go out there and ride like hell."

"Good advice."

Relief and excitement flood through my nerves. This is just what the doctor ordered: a good, healthy dose of my girl, Glory.

Chapter Ten

Stage 3: Sausalito to Santa Cruz, 116 Miles

I'm awakened by the hiss of tires on wet asphalt. More rain today. Chimes announce an incoming text. I check the time on my phone: 7:30. The message is from Dash: "COME TO ROOM 426 ASAP."

I look over at Armand, flat on his back, his open mouth emitting a disgusting sound that's halfway between a snore and a gargle.

"ARMAND?" I ask in a return text.

"JUST YOU."

I slip on some sweats and jog down the hall. The elevator is taking too long, so I use the stairs, something a sensible bike racer would never do. There's a spring to my step. Today's the day! I'm rested and ready to go!

Only Dash, Bernard, Mike, and Rainier are present in room 426. What's the big secret, I wonder.

"This is your big stage, Evan. Are you ready?" asks Dash.

"Yep. I got it down: Sit in until the last climb up Bonny Doon. Sal and I attack, then you join us. We pace you to the finish line in Santa Cruz."

"Change of plans," says Dash. "You've got to do it all on your own."

"I do?" My mouth goes dry. "What about Sal?"

"Duh," says Bernard. "Dash can't have the yellow jersey along with him if he's expecting to ride into it."

"Oh, . . . yeah, huh?" My nape gets prickly, and I shift in my chair.

"We don't have to worry about Sal," says Dash. "Rainier already had a talk with him. He got his glory yesterday, a stage win and his day in the yellow jersey. He's satisfied with that. He's agreed to chase down any dangerous breakaways today that include Temir or Klaus and block them. He understands his place on this team. If something happens to me, and I can't win, then Sal can win. If Sal can't win, then Bernard can."

Bernard rears back his head, surprised to hear his own name.

Dash looks at Mike. "One way or another, Image Craft–Icon is going to bring in a win." He looks back at me. "Your concern is . . ."

"Bonny Doon." I give him a thumbs-up.

Everyone shakes hands or slaps backs or knocks knuckles, and that's it. The meeting is over, and I have a huge job on my shoulders. We go down to the dining hall to meet the rest of the team and staff for breakfast, but there's no sign of Armand.

I go back to our room and get ready. Occasionally I look over at Armand, his mouth as wide as a pothole. It's getting close to nine and time to board the bus. I slam things around as I pack my gear, hoping he'll stir, but still he goes on sawing logs. I sit on his bed and bounce up and down. "Armand! Get up! Time to go."

He mutters something in French, all swear words, I think, and clutches the blankets under his chin.

I yank the blankets off him. "Armand, we gotta go!"

He sits up and clutches his head in agony. "Oh! Oh! I am ill," he says in English. "The putrid wines of California poison me. The rains of sunny California pour on me. I leave California to Mickey Mouse. I quit this lousy Tour of California."

"You can't quit! Image Craft–Icon needs you!"

"Go away, Image Craft–Icon. I quit you!" He retrieves his blankets and settles down again.

I press my fingers to my brow, thinking. I text the single word "Help," hoping, hoping. Ten seconds tick by, thirty, forty-five, one agonizing minute. I'm about to try again when my phone rings. I go out in the hall to answer it.

"Evan, what's the matter? Are you hurt?"

"How come it's all echoey?"

"What do you think?" says Glory. "I'm in the girls' room." Arizona is one hour ahead of California, so it's around ten there, and of course, she's at school.

"Do they call it a girls' room even at an all-girls' school? I mean, like, is there even a boys' room?"

"Evan! What? I'm going to get detention for talking on the phone in here."

"I need you to talk French to Armand sooner than I expected."

Glory lets out a puff of air. "I wasted my only bathroom pass of the semester for this?"

"No, listen. This is serious! He's hungover, and I can't get him out of bed. We can't afford to lose a team member this early in the race."

"What could I possibly say to him?"

"Just be yourself. You could charm the pants off any guy. Wait, no, that came out wrong. And be sure to say you're *my* girlfriend. I don't want him getting ideas. Just tell him you're a big fan of his."

"That would be a lie."

"Tell him you saw him in the race yesterday. You did see him. You just didn't know it was him."

There's a pause. "Put him on," she says.

"Thanks, babe. I so totally appreciate this!"

I go back into the room and place my phone against Armand's ear. "It's for you."

"*Moi? Qui est là?*"

"It's Glory."

I hear Glory rattling off French, giggling, then rattling some more. Whatever she's saying, Armand likes it. His eyes pop open. He sits up.

"Evan?" he says, and then something else, probably not complimentary.

Glory laughs.

Armand laughs.

Aren't they having a great time?

In another few minutes he hangs up and hands my phone back to me. "*Quelle fille charmante,*" he says, chuckling. He lifts himself out of bed and heads for the bathroom.

I get my stuff and hurry down to board the team bus. Bernard looks around at us, his chin bouncing as he seems to be counting heads. His eyes fall on me. "Will Monsieur Armand Fitzroy be joining us this morning?"

"Oh, yeah. He's coming," I say confidently.

Bernard turns to Dash. "Tell me again why we signed him on."

"We needed an eighth."

Bernard rubs beneath his bulbous nose. "What good is an arrogant domestique?"

"Don't call him that," says Dash, "at least not to his face. I mean, he is a domestique, and he knows it, but to get him to do all that pacing yesterday, I told him he was an integral player on our team."

"Integral player? You know those words in French?"

Dash grins. "I think I used the French word for star."

"Oh, shit." Bernard hits the heel of his palm against his brow as we all laugh.

Armand finally appears, shakily mounting the steps of the bus, and we head for Sausalito. It's raining, of course. On the Golden Gate Bridge the wind pushes against the bus, and I wonder how that will feel on a bike. Is it possible for the whole peloton to be swept into the bay?

The race begins near a harbor filled with sailboats, their bare masts like Aspen tree trunks. As we turn onto Bridgeway, Angel Island appears in the foreground, with the silhouette of the Bay Bridge and San Francisco skyscape in the distance. Our entourage of cars piled with bikes, motorcycles laden with bicycle wheels and camera equipment, and 123 cyclists climbs out of Sausalito, approaching the Golden Gate Bridge.

I can see the distant orange tower contained perfectly in the lowest arch of the closer one. On the bridge we are battered by sheets of gray rain and the cold north wind. Our wheels kick up water that sprays our legs. Who can care about such misery while experiencing such a moment? This is the ultimate photo op, and here we are, Image Craft–Icon, front and center in the peloton, hovering around the wearer of the yellow jersey, who is not our team leader. If Dash is bothered by this, he certainly doesn't show it as he laughs and banters with Bernard.

In San Francisco we meander through the Presidio and pass a stand of leaning cypress trees. The neutral zone ends as we drop down twisty Lincoln Avenue and pass pastel row houses on El Camino del Mar and Clement Street. We roll over short, steep ascents and plunge down inclines made narrow by crowds of spectators.

We turn onto the Great Highway and pass Cliff House and the windmill at the foot of Golden Gate Park. Along the surf's edge we roll at a manageable 25 mph pace, which would be quite pleasant if it weren't for the rain and the cracks in the pavement jarring our hands, feet, and asses every three feet.

We pass the zoo and Lake Merced, then turn onto Highway 1, bordering the ocean. The route to Santa Cruz offers no shelter from the pounding wind and punishing rain. No one gets away on the flats, and as we near the outskirts of Pacifica the sprinters charge to the front on the wheels of their teammates, who lead them out. Our sprinter, Charles, selects Armand's wheel and jockeys for position. Having punctured early on yesterday, he had no chance to earn sprint bonuses toward the green jersey and is eager to try his luck today. I'm glad that Charles is having a better day and impressed that Armand can perform so well with a hangover. The rest of our team holds back to give the sprinters plenty of room to fight it out.

Nearing the green banners that mark the sprint line, the front riders rocket out of their saddles and pound the pedals. Charles comes around Armand an instant before Armand spews projectile vomit first on one side of his bicycle and then on the other. The victims of the attack groan and curse as their bicycles clash in the commotion, but miraculously everyone stays up. Is barf a sort of tactic? If so, it worked. Charles wins the sprint while Dash and Bernard nearly laugh their asses onto the asphalt.

Those riders hardest hit by Armand drift to their team cars to get cleaned up. Armand fastidiously rinses his mouth with his water bottle and reclaims his position with his team, not a fleck of gunk on him, gazing about in his snooty way. A rider could hold a grudge against him and may accidentally-on-purpose hook his rear wheel into Armand's front one. When the second sprint comes up in Half Moon Bay, Dash orders Joris to lead Charles out.

This time Charles places third in the sprint. Eight of the dozen or so riders who contested the sprint keep pouring it on, and with that many guys working together, the break-away quickly obtains a 1:30 gap. By mile forty the gap widens to 2:40. I look at Dash, who seems unconcerned; no one in the break is a threat. At mile 44 the route leaves Highway 1 to turn onto Tunitas Creek Road for a 34-mile loop, northwest of Palo Alto. A six-mile Category 2 climb leads to the first of two King of the Mountains climbs for the day.

The suddenly narrow road squeezes the peloton into a tighter bunch. The surface is patched and bumpy, which is bound to cause more flats. The climb begins gently through open grassland dotted with residences and horse ranches. After several miles we enter a forest, the swollen Tunitas Creek roaring through it.

When the climb gets serious with grades as steep as 11 percent, Sal rolls off the front. Dash and Bernard look at each other as if to say he's not supposed to do that. Within a few miles Sal bridges the gap. Now the breakaway is dangerous.

"Evan, go get him," says Dash.

Block a teammate? That seems ludicrous, but I jump into attack mode. A couple of guys try to go with me, but soon give up. Sal's blistering pace has shattered the breakaway. Instead of members of a well-tuned paceline, the riders trail down the mountainside. As I pass each of them their faces exhibit various stages of exhaustion. My core is a furnace; my fingers are icicles. With a tremendous push I catch Sal. I position myself in front of him and slow down.

"Evan, you no help!" he exclaims.

Doesn't he get it? He's going against the orders of our *directeur sportif,* so I've been sent to hold him back.

"Evan, move away!"

I do. I mean, it's just too weird to block a teammate. I drop behind him, and soon I feel like he's going too slow. I'm pedaling squares, jerking the pedals so slowly, they come to a complete stop before my next stroke. Using a smaller gear, Sal dips one shoulder, then the other, leaning hard on the pedals, but not giving out much power. His yellow jersey is soaked and sticking to his skin. A brown smear streaks down his back where his rear wheel has flung mud.

I steer around him. He looks glassy-eyed and haggard. All the attacking he did yesterday has taken its toll. I'm out of here! I jump on my pedals and give them a good, strong revving up. It feels great to be out of the saddle, dancing the bike up the incline.

Rainier comes on my radio, "Back off, Evan. Save it for later."

"Just let me get up the mountain. Slow climbing hurts my knees."

I hear Mike laughing and clapping his hands in the background.

"Okay, go for it," says Rainier, "but take it easy on the descent. There's no reason to take risks."

"Right." I dig into the pedals. It stops raining. The sunlight shoots between the trees, lighting the drenched tops of the foliage a glimmering silver. The forest thins, so that between the branches I can see the expanse of the Pacific Ocean below me. My girl's beautiful face pops into my mind, and I think, Oh, Glory, look at me now. I break into song: "Glory, glory, hallelujah! Glory, glory, hallelujah!"

The spectators grow thicker. I look back and see no sign of Sal, only the curve of the road. I look ahead and see the King of the Mountains banner flapping in the wind. This is the best moment of my life! I'm the lead guy in a stage of the Tour of California! The fans hoot and whistle as I pass under the banner to capture King of the Mountain points. I shift into my highest gear, accept the gift of newspaper from a fan, and crouch into position for a leisurely descent.

That doesn't last for long. The climb isn't over yet. I'm faced with a few more switchbacks before reaching Skyline Boulevard. Although I've climbed only 1,500 feet above sea level, the cool air makes it feels like I'm in the mountains. I take on a series of rollers before plunging down toward the sea. The road is wide, the surface smooth. With traffic blocked off and no other riders around, I'm free to choose my own path down the highway, a fairly straight line down the center, as the yellow line curves beneath my wheel first to the right, and then to the left, alternating down the incline.

At the bottom, I follow the lead car left onto Highway 1 with the assistance of a California Highway Patrol officer, who is stopping traffic. I coast along the ocean shore until I'm caught by the peloton, Dash and Bernard gliding up beside me.

"What are you doing, my young buckaroo?" Dash asks.

I can't think of a good excuse for not following his orders. My answer comes out hesitantly and lame. "I'm just . . . um . . . riding my bike."

"You just had to ask," Bernard says.

"You were supposed to be my secret weapon," says Dash. "Now everyone knows what you've got. You do still got it, don't you?"

"I think so."

"You *think* so? I thought I sent you up there to block Sal."

"He didn't like it."

Bernard hoots and slaps his knee.

"Sal said, 'Move away,' so I did, and then he just, like, faded. A steep grade like that, I gotta have some momentum to get up it."

Both Dash and Bernard roar with laughter like I'm a stand-up comedian. Somehow, it seems, I'm forgiven.

The peloton passes San Gregorio Beach, where a few surfers in their wet suits appear like seals in the waves. The sun begins to dry the road. The relaxed pace doesn't last for long. Just after Pescadero, another break of seven riders launches off the front.

"Go get 'em, Evan," says Dash.

No one in the break is dangerous. We've only passed mile eighty; the finish line is 36 miles away. I don't get why Dash wants me to attack now, but I do, without further discussion.

I bridge the gap in a couple of minutes. Now that I'm in the breakaway, I'm not sure what to do. I know Dash is supposed to join me on the Bonny Doon climb, but that's 25 miles down the road. I drop into the last position of the paceline, pull through, and take my turn bucking the wind up front, just to be polite.

When I peel off and take the back position again, I speak to Rainier on my radio.

"Should I do my share of the work?"

"How do you feel?"

Worried. Unsure. "Fine."

"We want this break to gain some ground, but your major workload comes later."

"Got it." I hope I got it. Right now, I'm wishing I wasn't so cocky on the Tunitas Creek climb.

There are some pretty strong riders in the breakaway, and all of them are willing to work. The Image Craft–Icon team car and three others pull in behind us. It's not always easy to get a team car around the peloton and up to a breakaway on narrow roads. Now ours is perfectly positioned for Dash to attack on Bonny Doon.

Over the next twenty miles the break steadily widens the gap to five minutes. I'm getting tired and worried that I won't have enough gas left in the tank for Bonny Doon. My next pull is short and halfhearted.

"What the hell was that?" one Vision Tech rider yells at me. "We gotta get as far ahead as we can now if we're going to beat Dash on the climb."

"You moron," says a second Vision Tech rider. "He's working for Shipley."

"Why don't you work with us," says the first guy, "and grab something for yourself?"

A stage win? I'm not tempted. I'm here for Dash, and besides, I couldn't outsprint these guys if I tried. The guys in the break badger me some more, so I do a little more work. As we approach Santa Cruz the rolling hills are longer and steeper, and two guys in the breakaway slide off the back. Finally we turn onto Bonny Doon Road, which is narrow and bumpy but fairly level at first. By then, our lead has decreased to a little over three minutes. The peloton is pouring it on.

We leave the open terrain and enter a pine forest, the branches on either side of the road touching overhead, creating a dark, misty tunnel. It's not exactly raining, but the air is wet and so is the twisty road. Spectators beneath their umbrellas dot the side of the road, increasing in numbers higher up the mountain. I rise out of my saddle and push the pace. Several more riders drop off the back; now only two are hanging with me. Where's Dash?

Below me the crowd roars.

"Dash attacked!" Mike calls excitedly over my radio. "This is it, Evan! You ready?"

"Yeah." I increase my pace and burn off the last two riders in the breakaway. Every couple of seconds I look beneath my arm checking for Dash's approach. Finally he appears, passing the riders dropped from the breakaway like they're standing still. He is truly beauty in motion. With every turn of the cranks, his bike seems to jump ten feet. I've never seen such strength in a climber. Now I know why he wanted me positioned so far up the mountain before he made his move.

He passes the rider just below me, gently tapping him on the shoulder to make his presence known. I rev up, trying to match his pace. He grabs my wheel and here we go—up, up, up the mountain.

"Go, Evan!" Dash orders. "Faster! Drive us up to the summit."

My heart is yammering, my lungs are burning, my thighs are screaming in pain. Glory. Oh, Glory, I'm dying! "Glor-ry" I utter, my singing coming out like a groan. "Glor-ry, glor-ry, hal—"

"What is that ungodly sound?" Dash calls from behind me. "Jam it, Evan."

Super Heckler Man in his blue tights, red cape, and big Afro suddenly appears, running at my side, mimicking my groans in a bawdy, off-key parody. He staggers close, bumping my handlebars. I'm so pissed I want to ram an elbow into his face. The image of blood spurting out of his broad nose makes me feel better.

Just when I think I'm giving it my all, I dig in and find more power, stomping on the pedals and outdistancing the caped maniac beside me.

In our radios Rainier announces, "A chase group has formed: Temir, Klaus, Bernard, and Sal. Bernard and Sal are trying to block, but Temir and Klaus are moving pretty good."

I continue to climb, Dash on my wheel. Up ahead is the red King of the Mountains banner. Dash does not bother to come around me to place first in the KOM points. He has set his sights on one thing—the GC win—and I earn top King of the Mountains points for the second time today.

We turn onto Empire Grade Road, preparing for the plunge into Santa Cruz. I hear the clack of Dash shifting into high gear as he comes around me. "Follow my line on the descent, and don't be a grandma about it. Take some gulps of air and try to rest."

How can I rest with my heart in my throat? Having the road to ourselves, Dash can choose the shortest route through the twists in the road. He's known to ride aggressively on descents, and I'm worried I'll be left behind. I try to be brave, laying the bike down on one side, then the other, nearly scraping my pedal. One false calculation on the slick road will cause a wipeout. I concentrate on Dash's wheel and hang on.

He gets a little ahead of me, but nearing the base of Empire Grade near UC Santa Cruz, he coasts, allowing me to catch up. It seems we're nearly done, but I know the finish is still six miles away, and it's my job to tow Dash to the line.

We turn onto High Street, and I take the front position. I put my head down and go all out. Santa Cruz is a hilly town, so we still have more work to do. We pass through a residential area, fans cheering and clapping on every porch and driveway. Dash takes a couple of short pulls up front, but it's mainly me, driving us toward the line. We swerve onto the main drag, Mission Street, and head into the downtown area on Pacific Street. Here's our last turn, Front Street, where the raucous fans behind the yellow Tour of California banners are a dozen deep. After over five hours of racing, the finish line is just ahead!

Now is the time Dash needs to blast around me to take the stage win.

Something's wrong. Where is he? I stop pedaling. A firm hand shoves my back. Is a crazed fan trying to knock me down? I hold steady, and beneath my bike I see the blur of the finish line.

"Stick your arms in the air, Evan!" exclaims Dash. He has awarded me the stage, a gift for working for him.

I can't believe it! I'm the winner of a stage in the Tour of California! "Glory, hallelujah!" I shout as I take my victory ride past all the screaming fans.

The chase group comes in one minute twenty-seven seconds later, followed by the peloton. Our plan worked! I accomplished what I had been hired to do! I led Dash up Bonny Doon and into the yellow jersey! That puts Dash one minute twenty seconds ahead of Klaus in the GC standings, enough to keep him in the lead the rest of the race.

Max runs up to me, helps me dismount my bicycle. He wipes some of the grit off my face and combs my hair. "Gotta look pretty for the podium," he says.

The podium.

I am first up as the stage winner. One podium girl hands me the California brown bear and the other one, an especially hot girl with brown hair and a glint in her wide brown eyes, hands me a bouquet. Together they kiss my cheeks. Now I'm supposed to throw the bouquet into the crowd, but something makes me tighten my grip on it, and I can't let go. The moment passes, and I'm led off the stage.

Next Dash bounds on stage to wriggle into a spanking fresh yellow jersey. The winning sprinter claims the green jersey, Sal still leads in overall KOM points and gets a fresh red King of the Mountains jersey, a young rider claims the white jersey, and then comes my second shock of the day.

Over the loudspeaker the commentator announces, "For his role in two aggressive breakaways, the capture of both KOMs of the day, and the stage win, Evan Boroughs is awarded the blue Most Courageous Rider's jersey."

Glory, hallelujah!

Up to the podium I go for the second time. More flowers, more kisses, a blue jersey falls neatly over my arms as if it were made for me.

Through the crush of team members, team staff, TV crews, and fans comes a serious-looking man with a white lab coat draped over an impressive paunch. "Mr. Shipley, Mr. Boroughs, we'll need a few minutes of your time. Follow me, please."

I look over at Dash, and he shrugs. "It's routine. All race leaders and stage winners are drug-tested as well as a few other random guys. You're clean, right?"

"Well, yeah."

"Nothing to worry about then."

But somehow I feel dirty, like getting arrested for shoplifting and wondering if something like a diamond ring just happened to drop into my pocket. I think back on all the stuff I've ingested in the past several weeks. Cold medicine, a poppy seed bagel, food or drink someone handed me—is there anything that could cause me to test positive?

As we're led away to the drug-testing trailer I overhear a spectator say, "Gotta be a reason why a young kid like that can go so fast. He even looks guilty."

I stop and turn, thinking what I can say to defend myself.

Dash presses the heel of his hand into my back to keep me moving. Inside the trailer, I'm asked to drop my shorts and pee in a cup while the technician watches. Then it's Dash's turn. Walking back to the team bus, Dash kids me about how long it took me to produce.

"Well, it's not easy with some strange guy staring at my dick," I complain.

Dash laughs. "You get used to it. I've been drug-tested like fifty times, and not just at races. Any time, any place the UCI can knock on your door and demand your piss or your blood, whatever they want. It's like part of the dues to belong to the club."

The UCI, or Union Cycliste Internationale, is the governing body of pro cycling. It's very powerful, and it decides if a rider can race or not. Some people claim that cycling has the biggest doping problem of any sport, and the UCI is always on it.

Dash claps my shoulder. "Congrats, Evan, on your first piss-in-a-cup."

That night in my San Jose hotel room, I'm lying on my bed in a semiconscious state. My whole body is still vibrating with the hammering I took on the road, but it's a good, satisfying kind of tired. I close my eyes and see the pounding surf, the green rolling hills, and the winding road. The pressure of the pedals is against my feet, and it feels like I can ride forever.

My phone ringing jolts me to reality, and I answer it on the third ring without checking the caller ID, certain it's my parents.

"Don't you know you're supposed to throw the bouquet?" asks Glory without even a hello.

I laugh. "I was saving it for you. It's Valentine's Day and—"

"Yesterday was Valentine's Day."

"Around Valentine's Day, and I had worked hard to earn those flowers. I didn't want just any girl to have them."

"How would you get them to me? They're probably wilting in your hotel room right now because you didn't put them in water."

"Uh-huh."

"Evan, the TV cameras were on you like the whole day. You were so hot up there on the podium, and one of those glam girls tried to bite your face off."

I laugh at Glory's concern over a podium girl's peck on the cheek. "She's old enough to be my mother."

"Eighteen-year-olds do not have twenty-something mothers."

"Jay does."

"That's a stepmother."

"A stage win, Glory, can you believe it? Wasn't Dash cool, shoving me over the line like that? All those years of staring up at his poster in my room, and now he's like part of my life."

"What does a stage win matter to him? Maybe he just wants to appear generous to build his fan base."

"'Course he wants to look like a good guy, but he *is* a good guy."

My weird, dreamy mood hasn't entirely faded. "Glory, what do you think of us living in a cozy little house in France like Lance Armstrong and his wife when he was first starting out? I'd wheel my bike out the front door to climb any mountains I could find while you went off to the University of Paris to work on your MD."

The pause on the line is uncomfortably long. "Didn't Lance and his wife get a divorce?"

"Yeah, but—"

"An MD earned in France wouldn't be valid in the States."

"It's just a dream, babe."

"I take it you're not abandoning the race."

Now she sounds like my mother. "As long as I'm useful to the team, I'll stick it out."

"I hope this doesn't hurt your grades. Can I talk to Armand?"

"Why?"

"It was fun to speak French with him. He's charming."

"He's not charming to any of us."

"Maybe he's lonely or homesick or—"

"Hungover? I don't want to talk about Armand."

She laughs. "Okay, babe. Tell me about your Most Courageous Rider jersey."

"It's soft and sleek. I find myself petting it like a cat. It's as blue as your beautiful eyes."

"Are you going to frame it?"

"Nope, I'm going to wear it. I'm going to wear it out, and then I'm going to wear it some more."

A few minutes after Glory and I hang up, Dad calls. "Awesome ride, son. We're so proud!"

"Thanks, Dad."

"The blue jersey is icing on the cake! I actually thought you might be wearing white today."

"Not even close, Dad. I lost a lot of time yesterday."

"Well, a stage win in the Tour of California—that's even better!"

Mom comes on and says, "Congratulations."

"Gee, thanks, Mom. When are you going home?"

"Tomorrow. Same as you."

Ah, hell. I have to remind her that I never promised to quit the race after Stage 3. "I ordered my cap and gown. What difference does it make if I prance around in it in the stadium or our backyard?"

"Oh, Evan, don't be sarcastic. I'll never forget how thrilling it was to see Meredith graduate."

"I remember it was long, boring, and hot as hell."

"You're being vindictive, Evan. I just don't understand how you would throw away your graduation on a silly bike race. I never imagined you could be this selfish."

She hangs up. I imagine all my classmates throwing their mortar boards in the air while I watch from the bleachers. It hurts just to think about it, but what my mom said to me hurts more: vindictive and selfish. That's me? I thought I was most courageous.

Chapter Eleven

Stage 4: San Jose to Modesto, 121 Miles

"GLORY HALLELUJAH" reads the headlines of the *San Jose Mercury News*, and suddenly I'm famous. Below the large print is my finishing photograph, my fingertips touching the sky, my head arched back, my mouth wide open. The article calls me "enigmatic," "charismatic," "unassuming," "a breath of fresh air in professional cycling."

My initial response is embarrassment, and the razzing I take from my teammates makes it worse. Everyone but our late riser, Armand, is at breakfast, gathered around a table in the hotel's dining room. We're quite colorful, with Dash in the yellow jersey, Sal in red, and me in blue. Bernard gives a dramatic reading of the newspaper article in various accents, including Cockney, Russian, Indian, and French while my teammates and support staff reel with laughter.

Glory has already sent me a photo of a cluster of people trampling over her front yard this morning with signs reading, "Glory, come out!" She didn't text a comment, but I know she isn't happy about it. I went online to leave her an apologetic message on Facebook, and her page is gone!

On the way to breakfast, I had to push through a crowd in the hotel lobby, signing autographs as I went, with fans shouting, "We love you, Evan." One pretty girl in a skimpy top and short skirt leaped into my arms and said, "Glory's not here. Will I do?" I tried to act casual about prying her off me, but it was awkward, video cameras rolling and cameras flashing.

Now Bernard is pumping his arms over his head holding the newspaper. I look around at the laughing faces of my teammates and forget about being embarrassed. It's a great moment despite today's impending 121-mile ride in the rain, wind, and cold.

I stand to get more eggs and potatoes off the buffet, and my knees buckle, so that I plop back down, knocking against the table and causing Bernard's coffee to slosh over his cup.

"Easy there, Fresh Air," he says.

"Legs a little fatigued?" Dash asks me.

"They feel like gummy worms."

"We won't give you much to do today, Evan," says Rainier. "Sit in and rest."

I nod, although I know even sitting in the peloton will be grueling. We're faced with two climbs, one being our first Category 1 climb. Categories are assigned to ascents based on the gears of an old car: the steepest climbs require first gear.

"Stay out of the crashes," says Dash, as if there's some way I can actually control that. "There will be plenty today, maybe some serious ones."

"My god, yes," says Rainier. "Calaveras Road has over forty hairpin turns, and the pavement will be slick."

There's a loud commotion, shrieks, and applause as Klaus Grunwald makes his entrance into the dining room. Klaus actually looks more Italian than German. He's short and dark, like Hitler without the mustache, rather than a typical blond, blue-eyed Aryan-race dude.

"We're wearing all sorts of jerseys today," says Bernard.

Klaus is sporting the rainbow jersey of a world champion. It's pure white, with thin bands of blue, red, black, yellow, and green encircling the chest. A rider has to get permission to wear a jersey other than his team's, and this is a tactic to undermine Dash's wearing yellow.

Dash glares at his previous teammate, his eyes narrowed.

"You hate that guy, no?" asks Sal.

"Not at all," Dash says easily. "I just want to beat him. When we were teammates, I never got the chance to prove I'm the better man."

"Here's your chance," says Bernard.

"Yep, I plan on wearing yellow the rest of the race. All I have to do is keep him in sight. I'm even going to beat Mr. World Time Trial Champion in Solvang. I've ridden that course dozens of times this winter."

"So we've got nothing to worry about," says Mike.

"Right. With the help of the best team here, I'm going to win the TOC." Dash looks around our table and smiles his self-assured, toothy smile. His business manager really ought to get him a toothpaste commercial.

It's raining. Again. The wind is up, and I shiver as I straddle my bike waiting for the start in downtown San Jose. We parade through the town in a three-mile neutral zone until we get the green light on Thirteenth Street. We don't even get a chance to warm up before we turn onto Sierra Road at mile four.

Soon the peloton is strung out, with the leaders and their teams at the front, Bernard and Sal acting as Dash's two main domestiques. This Category 1 is going to hurt, with grades as steep as 17 percent. We quickly rise in elevation, up and over the green hills of east San Jose, leaving the sprawl of Silicon Valley far below. A climb this steep usually works to my advantage, but today I'm suffering with everyone else. I look ahead hoping for a dip in the road or a lesser incline, but all I can expect is pure misery. I rise out of the saddle, hoping to feel better once I'm warmed up, but I can't find my rhythm, and it's just a miserable slog up the mountain. Churning the cranks doesn't come naturally. I have to send frequent memos from my brain to my legs to keep them moving. I find myself slipping back in the peloton, realize I'm in the back quarter, then push harder to battle my way to the front again. Before I know it, I'm sliding back and have to struggle to the front again. This happens three or four times; I lose count.

Spectators scream at me, "Go, Evan, go."

"Faster, faster."

"You can do it!"

You try it, I want to answer back. They mean well, but their encouragements sound like taunts. Here he comes, damn it, Super Heckler Man, flying into view to run at my side. He walks Groucho Marx–style, with his back arched and his hands clasped behind him to indicate how slow I'm going. I try to speed up to drop him, but the incline is too steep.

At last the road flattens out a bit and I gain momentum. Super Heckler Man has to run to keep up with me. His red cape snapping in the wind sounds like thunderclaps. Abruptly the sound stops, just as something stops my cranks from turning. A corner of the material is caught in my rear wheel.

I reach back to yank it out. My front wheel twists to the side. I'm going down!

Steady hands catch my fall. Several spectators have stepped out of the crowd to hold me up.

Super Heckler unwinds his cape from my spokes. "Sorry, Evan," he says, his moon-shaped face, caked with white makeup, inches from mine.

I want to say screw you but clench my teeth instead.

He offers me a newspaper, my photo on the front, and I bat it away. I'd rather have the wind bore a hole through me than take anything from this asshole.

"Oh, sore loser," he says. "Loooser."

"Newspaper!" I yell, "newspaper." A fan runs up and hands me one, and I tuck it under my jersey.

Descending, I see row after row of hills in such vast wilderness, it's hard to believe millions of people live nearby. The road narrows to a single lane causing the peloton to thin out to a long, twisty worm. Short guardrails are set where the drops are the longest, and there's no margin of error on either side of the road. As I swirl down the technical switchbacks of Calaveras ambulance sirens echo in the distance. I count the fallen riders crumpled in the wet curves: one . . . two . . . three is flipped over a guardrail . . . four.

I shimmy down the hill. The riders regroup as Calaveras makes a sharp turn north toward Livermore. I'm about in the middle of the pack, and see my team up ahead, controlling the front. I count heads, or rather red-and-blue backs plus Sal's red and Dash's yellow ones. They're all here. I fight my way up to them through the peloton. Joris is guarding Dash's wheel, and I slip in behind Bernard.

"Oh, hell, Dash, you've got a soft tire," Joris says.

"I feel it." Dash raises his right hand to signal that he's flatted. He drifts to the side of the road, and our whole team stops with him. Dash calls into his radio for help, but our team car is nowhere in sight. The race caravan had to pull over to let the ambulances through. Bernard and Joris jump off their bikes. Joris flicks through his gears, tugs on the quick release, and pulls his rear wheel out of his frame. Bernard has done the same to Dash's rear wheel, which he hands to Joris. Bernard places Joris's rear wheel on Dash's bike and secures the quick release.

We're off again in a pace line to tow Dash back to the peloton while Joris is left behind to wait for help. Taking advantage of our bad luck, the teams Kronen and Taraz have pushed the pace, and by now the peloton is far down the road, a splotch in the distance.

We put our heads down, preparing for the chase, but something's wrong. Dash's chain doesn't engage neatly with the rear sprockets of Joris's borrowed wheel but occasionally skips and bumps over the teeth. We limp along until Pablo roars up in a team car. He supplies Dash with a whole new bike.

We get our seven-man train rolling, each of us taking short, fierce turns up in the front, bucking the wind for Dash. Bernard's and Sal's pulls are especially bullish. When it's my turn, I go all out, but it's not enough.

"Pull over," Bernard growls behind me.

I'm not doing my team any good. After I drift back to the rear position, I struggle to maintain contact with Dedrick's wheel before me. A four-inch gap opens, a foot, two feet. Don't let go! I leap out of the saddle to regain contact. I find that sweet spot in the slipstream where riding seems effortless. "Wheel sucking," it's called. I even get a chance to coast. Then Armand peels off the front and Sal picks up the pace. I drift back again. Armand slips into the position in front of me so if I slip off the back, he won't be left behind, too.

Hold on, I coach myself between clenched teeth. *Hold on, hold on, hold—damn!*

I'm blown off the back. Heaving and puffing, I watch my team ride away without me. Only 27 miles into a 121-mile stage, and it feels like I've been riding all day. I'm stranded, out in the middle of no-man's-land, left to time trial my way in, not knowing if I'll ever see my team or the peloton again today. I suck on an energy gel and take a drink, but it seems nothing is going to help these dead legs.

After five miles or so, Mike radios me. "Evan, do you want to abandon?"

"No," I mutter weakly.

"You sure? You did what you set out to do yesterday. No reason to suffer now."

He's saying I'm no use to the team anymore. I only need to say the word, and in a few minutes I'll be whisked into a warm car with the heater blasting away. I could be on a plane to Phoenix in a matter of hours and sitting in a classroom tomorrow. Wouldn't that make my mom happy? I'd get to walk at graduation after all. I'd have Glory in my arms tonight. "I want to stick it out, Mike."

"Okay, Evan. It's your call."

That's cool. I know most team managers would be ordering: get in the car. You're done. "How is the team doing?" I ask.

"Almost to the peloton, but Klaus and Temir have launched an attack, and the gap is about two minutes."

Not good. I'm chasing my team, which is chasing the peloton, which is chasing a dangerous breakaway. I struggle along, hoping I'll be stronger tomorrow.

A dropped PolyTech rider in bright orange glides past me and I jump on his wheel. He glances back at me but says nothing. After a couple of minutes he peels off and I take the front position. We continue to share the work in silent agreement.

As we're trading pace, my companion gives me a hard look. "Aren't you the guy who won the stage yesterday?" he asks in American English.

"Yep."

He laughs. "That's bike racing. It's humbling."

"That's for sure." I explain about Dash's flat, how I couldn't keep up with my teammates' tempo.

"At least you've got an excuse. I can't climb worth shit."

We pass another dropped rider, a member of Doyle Cycling Team in a white jersey with green shamrocks, who falls in behind us. "I tink you're having a bad day, Evan."

He knows my name! An Irish rider, sounds like, but I don't know him.

"Is Dash as good a guy as he seems?" asks the PolyTech rider.

"Yeah. He was sure good to me yesterday."

"Do you tink he's clean?" asks the Irishman.

"Course he is," says the PolyTech rider. "He's passed every drug test, hasn't he? The French! They hate it when an American wins the TDF."

"It's not the French," says the Doyle rider. "'Tis everybody. People don't admire heroes today; they look for ways to take them down. It don't matter what sport. 'Tis true for the film stars, too. Just take 'em down and tank the Lord for it."

We fall silent as we strain to make contact with the peloton near the city limits of Livermore. We become separated in the pack as I try to work my way to the front. I never caught their names, but the camaraderie of those guys really boosted my morale.

There's a sprint coming up, but no one in the peloton contests it. The points have already been claimed by the members of Klaus and Temir's breakaway. When I get to the front, I only find Joris, Charles, and Armand. The rest of the team is off chasing Klaus.

The peloton is clicking along the flats at 26 mph. No one sees any reason or is in any mood to press the pace. Charles and Armand converse in French. Joris makes jokes about his brother, Dedrick, who is always putting the moves on women that frequently end in humiliation. He goes on to say he's had the same girlfriend since high school and would like to get married, but he can't afford it. Pros who don't earn bonuses by winning races don't make much money.

We're having so much fun shooting the breeze, I feel guilty, knowing how much Bernard, Dedrick, Sal, and Dash are suffering. I'm not too worried, though. It's true Klaus and Temir are eating away the lead that Dash and I sweat blood to obtain yesterday, but Dash should hold on to yellow today, if only by seconds.

We climb the second KOM of the day, a 1,500-foot Category 4. It's not too long and not too steep. It feels good to be out of the saddle, giving my aching ass a rest. It's strange, but the more miles I ride today, the better I feel.

After the descent it's a long, flat fifty-plus miles to Modesto. Apparently some of the riders just want it over with because they set a searing pace. I duck down my head and concentrate on Joris's rear wheel. Over my radio, I hear Rainier and Dash discuss their failed attempts to catch the breakaway. At mile 97 the swift peloton absorbs Bernard, Sal, and Dash, their faces covered in sweat, grit, and defeat. When the peloton cruises over the finish line in Modesto, we get word that the yellow jersey has a new owner, with 37 seconds to spare.

All our hard work yesterday is totally wasted.

As he watches Klaus ascend the podium Dash is visibly stunned. "I gotta do something about this."

"You will, bro, you will," says Bernard.

"I'll need some help, though," says Dash through clenched teeth. "Lots of extra help."

"Easy now." Bernard claps him on the shoulders, but Dash shrugs him off. I've never seen Dash treat him that way. I've never seen Dash lose his cool.

Before I get a chance to call Glory, she calls me. We've moved to our hotel in Merced, and I'm walking down the hall to our team dinner in the restaurant.

"Oh, sweet!" I answer. "Am I glad to talk to you!"

"Me, too. I've got some amazing news!"

"Yeah? I hope it's something to cheer me up. I just suffered through the most miserable day of my life!"

She hesitates. "Why? What's wrong?"

"You don't know Dash lost the yellow jersey?"

"Um, no. It's been kind of crazy around here and—"

"That big lead I helped him gain yesterday is gone! Wasted! And my legs were empty today. Mike suggested I abandon."

"You're coming home?" asks Glory, all excited.

"No! I can't believe you haven't been following the race."

"Sorry, babe. There's been so much going on."

"Oh, yeah. All those people trampling your yard. Sorry about that."

"It's okay." Her voice is high-pitched and girly. "Listen, you'll never believe it."

"What about your dad? Is he mad?"

"Oh, no. He went right out there and started talking to the TV reporters. Of course, he wouldn't say anything personal about us, what they really wanted to know, but he was bragging about you like crazy."

"He was?"

"Mom said when he watches you on TV, it's almost like—well, when Hunter won sailing competitions, he acted like that, too. What I really what to tell you—"

"I know. A bunch of people are stalking you, and I know how much you value your privacy. You took down your Facebook."

"I was going to anyway. It's a big waste of time and sort of sick—people spying on each other. Hey, know where Facebook got started?"

It seems like a silly, random question, but I answer, "Harvard."

"Right! That's what I've been trying to tell you, babe. I got accepted to Harvard!"

I sink into a nearby chair, my legs unable to hold me up another second. I'm a self-absorbed idiot for forgetting my brilliant, beautiful girlfriend has a life of her own.

"Evan? You there?"

"Con-congratulations! Wow, Glory! That's fantastic. You're going, aren't you?"

"Going? No! We have plans to attend UA together. But it's great to know I made the cut. I didn't really believe I could."

"You should think about it some more."

"There's nothing to think about. I want to be with you. It's going to be hell explaining that to my parents, but—"

"Tell them your real reason is to stay close to them."

She giggles. "That's a lie! They'd see right through that."

"But it's okay to lie to me," I say bluntly. How could I be so gullible? The Albrights look perfectly capable of taking care of themselves, and I know how ambitious they are for Glory.

She must not realize how angry I am because she giggles again. "I told Alfred you'd be smart enough to figure it out."

I leap to my feet and tread in circles. "Alfred? And I suppose he got accepted to Harvard, too."

"Well, yeah, but—"

"How come you keep throwing *Alfred* in my face?"

"I don't! I keep telling you, Evan. We're friends, and he needs me to talk to. He's been having trouble with his parents and well, if you just met him, you'd see—"

"I don't want to meet that shithead. I want you to stay away from him."

"Don't tell me who I can hang out with!" she snaps. "Like you don't have any friends that are girls?"

"I don't have any friends that are girls I *date*. I don't keep talking to you about others girls. You got accepted to Harvard, so go. Don't pass it up for my sake."

There's a silence, a sniffle. "Well, if we have to say good-bye in the fall, we might as well do it right now. You can forget about us and concentrate on your stupid Tour of California."

"It's not stupid, damn it. I guess that's something you'll never understand. You and Alfred just trot off to Harvard together, the golden couple."

There's a jagged sob as Glory breathes in. "You are so mean, Evan. Good-bye!"

I stand in the hall staring at my phone going beep, beep, beep. The Doyle rider I met today nudges my shoulder. "Hello, Evan. Someting wrong?"

"I think my girlfriend just broke up with me."

"You tink?"

"I tink."

He laughs. I laugh. Right now I'm too angry to be sad or sorry.

It's after nine, and I'm too stressed to sleep. I've got a sharp cramp in the arch of my right foot, so I decide to walk it out through downtown Merced. For about the tenth time since dinner, I pull out my phone and check it for a text from Glory. I'm not so angry anymore, and I really miss her. I wish I could've stopped my motormouth from spewing stuff I didn't mean.

I'm still can't believe Dash lost the hard-fought-for lead I helped him earn yesterday. At our team meeting Rainier discussed the plan of breaking away in the mountains tomorrow, and if we can't manage it, then Dash doesn't have much hope of winning the GC.

"Hi, Evan." A hot girl with long brown hair and wide eyes falls into step with me.

"Hey." I have to look up at her because she's about a head taller than me, mostly because of the heels she wears, with tight jeans and a low-cut, shiny top.

"You don't recognize me, do you? And I've already kissed you. I'm Kristee."

Her face is only half-illuminated by the streetlight. Some fans have run up and kissed me, but I don't remember this girl. She looks older than me, but not by much. "Kristee who?"

"Just Kristee."

"Everyone has a last name."

"Not Madonna. Not Beyoncé. And I have a distinctive spelling, with a double e. At first, I went by Kristi with an i, but I Googled it, and lots of girls end their names with an i, so I thought two e's would be more of a standout."

"Nice to meet you, Kristee with two e's."

"I told you, we've met. Here, let me refresh your memory." She stops me with her hand on my arm, then drops her face to plant a soft, warm kiss on my cheek.

"You're my podium girl! I guess I was in a state of shock and didn't notice too many details yesterday."

"I'm a detail?" She lays her fingers on her bare throat just above her sexy cleavage.

I laugh. "You know I didn't mean it that way. What do podium girls do when they're not . . . kissing?"

"I want to be a TV cycling commentator. Here, let me give you my card." She reaches in the back pocket of her jeans. "Shit, fresh out, but I've got more. I'll give you one tomorrow."

"Okay. It must be a tough business to break into."

"No kidding. I've got a communications degree, but that means nothing. I've been a weather girl—well, a substitute weather girl. I've raced, although I'm no good, but I still love to ride. I love everything about the sport. Right now I'm prowling around for good stories."

"Dash losing the yellow jersey is the top story today."

"That's not a story; that's a race report. Dash's story is donating that kidney to his son, the best thing that ever happened to his cycling career. As soon as the media picked it up, Kronen picked him up, and since then the 'family guy' image has kept him in the limelight."

"That's not a story. He really is a good family man."

She rolls her eyes.

"No, really."

"You don't have the insider's scoop. You must be too busy staring at the wheel in front of you to notice much else."

"That does keep me occupied." When we arrive at the entrance of my hotel, I add, "This is my stop."

"Oh, I'm staying here, too."

We enter the lobby. "I'd like to continue our conversation," I say, "but I better turn in."

"It's not that late. Let's have a beer."

Nothing like an ice cold beer to take the edge off and help me get to sleep. I look toward the bar. "I'd get carded."

"I've got some in my room."

The idea of a beer with this hot podium girl in her room

is exciting—not that I expect anything to happen between us, but the invitation eases the sting of Glory's rejection.

We continue to chat in the elevator. She swipes her key card at her door, lets us in, kicks off her heels with a groan, and slips into massive furry slippers. Clothes, shoes, and makeup are strewn all over the room. "Sorry, about the mess." She uncovers a couple of chairs at a table, removes two bottles of beer from a small refrigerator, pops them open, and hands one to me. We sit at the table and knock bottles with a satisfying clink.

"Cheers," says Kristee, and takes a pull. "You've got a great story going on, Evan, singing Glory! Hallelujah! at the top of your lungs while you ride. The *Merc* snatched it right up."

"I really do have a girlfriend named Glory. Well, had."

She raises her eyebrows, and her wide brown eyes seem to shoot even farther apart.

"Uh, we sort of broke up over the phone tonight. Ah, hell! I'm spilling my guts to the wrong person." I reach across the table and touch her wrist. "Please, Kristee! Don't make this public."

"I won't!" She slides her hand into mine and gives it a quick, reassuring squeeze. "Anything you say is completely off-the-record, I promise."

Her eyes are soft and sympathetic. I feel I can trust her, and yet rationally, I know I'm a fool to do it. But I need to confide in someone. "There isn't much to tell. I felt she misrepresented herself to me and then she mentioned this guy Alfred. She's always talking about him."

"You think she's cheating?"

I shrug. The thought had not occurred to me, not until now. "She's not crazy about me riding the TOC. Neither are my parents, especially my mom."

"That's just awful. All the pressures of the race and no support at home. It must be a lot of added stress."

I sigh deeply. "Yeah."

"I heard your mom had emergency surgery. Gallbladder, wasn't it? How's she doing?"

"Fine. How do you know?"

She shrugs, which gives her rack a lovely jiggle. She catches me gawking and looks back at me beneath lowered lashes. I go to take another swig, but the bottle is empty.

"Want another?"

"Sure. Tanks."

She laughs as she shuffles things in the refrigerator. "You've been talking to Timothy Malone."

"Who?"

"A Doyle rider. There's only two Irish riders here, and Sean Laird pronounces his *th*'s."

"My god, girl, you do know everything!"

"Oh!" She holds up a single beer. "There's only one left. You can have it."

"Naw, let's split it."

"Okay." I think she'll get glasses from the bathroom, but instead she opens the beer, takes a swig, plops down on the edge of the bed across from me, and hands over the bottle. As we continue to talk and trade off sips our mouths get closer and closer. I know exactly what's happening, and I let it. When we finally kiss, either she pulls me back onto the bed or I fall forward, I don't know exactly how it happens, but we're going horizontal, and it feels so good, I don't want to stop. I let it go on awhile before I push her gently away.

"I can't do this," I whisper. "I'm not sure what's going to happen with me and Glory."

"It's all good," she says cheerfully. "I better let you go,

then." Suddenly she sits up and swings her feet over the side of the bed, leaving a cold, empty spot next to me.

"Whoa, Kristee! Get back here!" I pull her down, nestle my head against her shoulder, and wrap her arm over me. "Ah, that's better. You feel so nice. Would you think I'm terrible for resting here just for a moment?"

"Not so terrible." She strokes my hair, running her fingernails around the back of my ear. Aaah, I just lie there, taking it in.

After a moment I murmur, "It isn't just Glory. It's everything. Dash losing today, and me taking a beating. The rain, the wind, the pace. It's so fucking hard, Kristee. I knew it would be, but not this . . ." I'm too exhausted to finish.

"You guys are so close to the breaking point most of the time."

Finally, a girl who understands. I close my eyes, just for a moment. "Hold me."

"My pleasure, Evan. You know, you really ought to have someone who supports your riding."

"Great idea," I whisper, black dots exploding in my head.

Chapter Twelve

Stage 5: Merced to Clovis, 116 Miles

Glory and I had this one little fantasy. We liked to plan spending the whole night together and waking up in each other's arms. It's my first thought when I open my eyes. I turn to the girl asleep next to me, and I'm about to kiss her when I realize she's not Glory.

"You let me stay the whole night?" I nearly shout.

Kristee's lids flutter open. "Well, good morning to you, too. You were sleeping so soundly, I didn't want to wake you, and then I fell asleep, and here we are."

"Oh, no! This can't be happening!" I exclaim. I sit up and vigorously rub my face. I'm still completely dressed, hoodie and all, except for my shoes, which have been removed sometime in the night. Kristee, I notice, has changed into flannel pajama bottoms and a long-john top, no bra.

"Chill, Evan. It's still early, not even eight."

"I'm sure I've been missed by now!"

Kristee sits up, clasps her arms around her legs, and rests her cheek on her knees. "Nothing happened."

I point to the door. "Tell that to them!"

Her head pops up like she's got an idea. "Why should we? Let them think what they want. It might make a good story."

"Oh shit, no. Please don't do that to me." I can just see the cycling blogs.

She laughs. "Your instincts are dead-on, Evan. Stick to the Glory story. It serves you better. It's a sweet story, and you're a sweet guy. I'll check the hall, then you can sneak out. First I gotta pee."

She disappears around a partition. I hear her using the bathroom without closing the door while I lace my shoes. She reappears, bounds out of the hotel room propping the door ajar, then pops back in. "Coast is clear. Oh! I almost forgot!" She rummages through several of her numerous bags, then hands me her business card. "You'll put in a good word for me when you can, won't you?"

"Sure, but I don't really know anybody who—"

"You'll see. In this sport, when you talk, people will listen."

"Thanks for the vote of confidence, Kristee. Thanks for, you know, everything."

"I didn't do anything."

I grip her shoulders. I have to tilt my chin slightly to look into her laughing brown eyes. "Yeah, you did. You did a lot."

"Want to hang out after the stage this afternoon? We can meet at Brewbakers in Visalia, this neat little microbrewery."

"Sure." When I kiss her good-bye, she pulls me close with the belt loops of my jeans, so that our bodies slam together.

I sprint out of the room, down the hall, and up a flight of stairs to my floor. Inside my room, my bed is still made and Armand is gone. I mess up the bed, change into my team kit, and rush down to the dining room for a late breakfast.

At the start line, the sun is shining behind the Merced Courthouse. Glory has dumped me, and with Kristee, this new, exciting woman in my life, I'm probably reeling toward disaster, but right now, I don't care. I feel great. I must be grinning like a lunatic because both Dash and Bernard give me strange looks.

"What's up with you, Sunny Boy?" asks Bernard. "You look like you got laid."

"Armand did happen to mention you weren't in the room when he woke up," Dash says suspiciously.

"I'm never in the room when Armand wakes up. We're usually halfway through the day's ride."

"True enough," says Bernard. "Besides, Sunny Boy's got a girlfriend back home, a Somebody Hallelujah. Right?"

"Right." I lie. "I just feel good is all."

"I'm glad someone does," says Dash.

"One hundred sixteen miles in the mountains ought to wipe that silly grin off your face," says Bernard.

Merced, almost at sea level, is known as the Gateway to Yosemite. We're not headed to Yosemite, but south of there, 3,650 feet up the Sierra Nevada, with five KOMs. It's in the cool fifties and most of the riders are wearing leg warmers, arm warmers, and vests, except for Temir, who wears only his shorts and jersey. I don't know what the weather is like in his native Kazakhstan, but like many pros, he lives and races in Europe most of the year and knows the chill of high mountain passes.

We roll off to a six-mile neutral zone, a figure eight through the downtown area, then head out of town. Beyond the green flag we follow a two-lane country road lined with blooming orchards. The roads are mostly dry, but there are oceans of puddles lapping over the shoulder and little lakes in the potholes. Who knows what debris is sunk in the muck? In a crowded pack, riders are expected to hold their lines to avoid a crash, which means someone has to splash through the potholes, and I imagine there will be a lot of flats today. Team Kronen is controlling the sharp end of the peloton, protecting the yellow jersey. Taraz and Image Craft–Icon follow behind, complacent to let Klaus's guys buck the wind for now.

Dash has gotten permission from Mike to wear the Stars and Stripes as National Road Champion rather than our team kit. He points out the blossoms on the trees and offers a running commentary. "The white ones are almonds," he says. "Those deep pink ones are nectarines."

"How do you even know shit like that?" asks Bernard.

"I can read."

As far as I know, Dash has only a high-school education. He must have been good in math because he's always talking about gear ratios, frame angles, lung volume, and power meter readouts. No racer can rise to the top merely on brute strength, and Dash is constantly analyzing data and racing smart.

There's a commotion in the center of the pack, and I look back to see a snarl of riders go down. The fallen riders who are able to continue take turns riding alongside the medical car, allowing the race doctor to lean out the rear window to clean and bandage their scrapes. The race doctor can call any injured or sick rider unfit to continue, and for that reason some riders who figure they have broken bones or a severe illness will steer clear of the doctor just to remain in the race.

The peloton jogs to the right and then the left, and at last we are on Highway 140 and a smooth surface. All around us is open land, with cattle and sheep grazing. In the distance is the Sierra Nevada, ominous clouds swirling around its summit.

At mile 22, as Klaus is shedding his vest Rainier says, "Now!" into our radios. Bernard, Sal, Charles, Dash, and I attack, while Joris, Dedrick, and Armand try to block. Down the road we organize ourselves into a paceline, motoring Dash up the first climb. Our gap increases to 45 seconds as we mount a series of rollers that grow longer and harder as we head toward the first King of the Mountains, a Category 3, 2,300-foot climb. Sal is first in KOM points, Bernard is second, and I'm third.

Our gap increases to 1:20, even though Klaus and Temir and their teams have formed a chase group. Could we possibly be on the winning break so soon in the stage? My own pulls are nearly as hard as the others. Calves screaming, back breaking, throat aching, I don't care if I blow myself up and have to limp in with the *gruppetto*; I'm serving Dash well when he needs me the most.

We enter the western-style town of Mariposa. Spectators gathered under awnings cheer us on. Charles surges ahead to easily take the sprint points, but we make a show of pretending to contest the sprint against our own sprinter, just to entertain the fans. Heading out of town on Highway 49 toward Bootjack, I feel sprinkles.

Bernard holds up his palm, looking up at the sky. "Of course. We can't ride a single stage in this damn race without it raining on us."

More bad news: the sprinkles turn into a hard, stinging rain.

More bad news: the chase group is effective. The gap is reduced to 50 seconds, then 35, then 17, and we're caught. Everyone settles down to a slower pace, and the peloton rolls in behind us.

"Good effort," Mike says over our radios. "Rest awhile, then go again."

The rain turns white.

"Is this hail or sleet?" I ask.

Dash laughs. "Snow!"

Temir, I notice, is shivering, while Dash seems to be enjoying the rotten weather, or at least is good at pretending to. As we continue to climb, the banks of snow and wall of spectators thicken. Fans begin to run beside us. I look for my nemesis Super Heckler Man, but don't see him. There's a banana and a pope. There's a pair of Sumo wrestlers who appear to be streaking nearly naked but in fact are wearing rubber fat suits. A guy with huge antlers runs directly in front of us. He can't really go as fast as the peloton and is getting in the way. Riders and fans yell at him to move. He veers slightly to the side directly in front of our team, and we press together as we go around him. Dash sticks out his broad hand and shoves the guy into a snowbank, face-first.

It's a popular move. Riders and fans alike enjoy the moment, everybody but Temir, who is now shivering so violently, he's about to shake himself off his bike. He summons his team car, and when it arrives, some of the Taraz staff leap out of the car, help Temir off his bike, and hustle him into the car.

"My god, is he done?" I ask.

Dedrick shrugs. "Probably just needs to thaw out."

Klaus sees his advantage and pushes the pace; Bernard, Sal, Charles, and Dash stick with him. The peloton begins to break apart due to the speed and road conditions. I try to go with the surge, but my rear wheel loses traction and I have to sit down to keep it from sliding out from under me. Riders are going down all around us. On a short descent after the second KOM, the road curves and Armand goes straight, smashing into a snowbank. He and his bike do a perfect flip, which would be great if this sport had an element of freestyle. He's thrown on his back in the snow, and his bike comes to a halt nearby, the rear wheel sticking up and still spinning.

"Nine point zero," says Joris.

"Eight point five," says Dedrick. "Did you see his hips twist? Bad form."

"You Dutch always score too low," I say. "A perfect ten."

Dedrick, Joris, and I applaud and hoot, then stop to help Armand.

It appears that he had a fairly soft landing and is all right. His main problem is that we're laughing at him.

He gets up spitting snow and flicking it out of his helmet. He grabs his bike and hurls it into a grove of pine saplings. *Je laisse tomber ce Tour de Californie. Je quitte cettee Californie et je quitte l'Amerique.*

"I think that means he's done," I say.

"Ja! Ja!" says Joris, nodding and laughing.

Pablo pulls up in our second team car and Armand gets in. Pablo dashes across the snow to unrack Armand's bike from the branches of the tree. It's bad we've lost a teammate, but we're still laughing.

It stops snowing as we trade pace up the third KOM. Soon Taraz comes, towing Temir, who has on leg warmers, jacket, fingered gloves, and a knit skullcap under his helmet. We slip into the back position of the Taraz train for a free ride to the peloton. Dash, Bernard, and Sal attack on the fourth KOM, the gap widens to 45 seconds, but they are again sucked back into the peloton by Klaus and his Kronen teammates.

The peloton, descending into Oakhurst, is shuffled again. After nearly three hours and sixty miles of hard riding, we are right back in the positions we started in, Kronen at the helm, Taraz and Image Craft–Icon right behind. Everything seems the same as it was, or is it? Who knows what each of the race leaders is feeling or how much strength remains in them?

Dash just gets fed up and dashes away on his own like a madman. With each flex of his muscled legs, the bike leaps farther up the final 3,650-foot climb, until he disappears behind a turn in the road. I look over at Bernard, whose mouth is a tight crease. Clearly, he doesn't approve. Temir, after his bout with hypothermia, is in no mood to chase.

Klaus sits up on his bike and laughs. "Idiot! *Dummkopf.* He really thinks that will work?"

Over our radios we hear Mike talking to Dash: "Are you sure you want to do this?"

"It's *done,*" says Dash.

Soon after that, our team car is able to pass the peloton strung out over the climb in order to support Dash's effort. By the time Dash crests the summit up ahead, the gap has opened up to two minutes. I can only image what kind of pain he's in. Maybe he's beyond pain, in the zone where it hurts so good, you can't even feel it anymore. But can he keep up this frenzied pace for another 45 miles?

Meanwhile, Klaus climbs steadily and sure, tucked in behind his strongest domestiques. He seems to think he has nothing to worry about. As the peloton climbs, Dash descends, increasing the gap to seven minutes.

Mike is ecstatic, shouting, "Go, Dash, go!" so loudly that I have to turn down my radio or go deaf.

The descent is an easy, sloping incline, which requires pedaling. Klaus and his Kronen teammates organize a chase at the front of the peloton, and those of us sitting-in just enjoy the ride. Soon the gap is down to four minutes.

"Come on, Dash," yells Mike.

"Yeah, Dasher, go," Bernard mutters next to me.

As we drop into the San Joaquin Valley the temperature

rises and steam rolls off our drying clothes. At mile one hundred we enter Fresno County, and soon we're weaving through the streets of Fresno and Clovis, fans crowding the sidewalks. The gap is less than two minutes, but the stage is coming to an end.

"Hey, Sauerkraut," Bernard yells at Klaus. "Save your energy. He's got you."

Klaus mutters obscenities in German between clenched teeth. He hunches over his bike, pedaling harder.

Through our earpieces and in the distance, we hear the roar of thousands of Dash fans as his stunning solo ride comes to an end. One minute 12 seconds later the peloton crosses the line, and the Tour of California has a new race leader.

Dash slips into a fresh yellow jersey at the podium ceremony. Kristee and the blond podium girl kiss him simultaneously on the cheeks, and he tosses his bouquet. As usual, as the stage winner and wearer of the yellow jersey Dash is lead off by the fat man in the white coat to the drug-testing trailer. What's not usual is that while I'm waiting at Brewbakers to meet Kristee, who incidentally never shows up, the news breaks that Dash's drug test is positive.

Chapter Thirteen

Stage 6: Visalia to Paso Robles, 134 Miles

First thing in the morning, Dash texts me, asking me to come to his room. I don't know how I can even look him in the face. When he opens the door, I think he's alone, but then I hear the shower running and assume Bernard is in there. Dash is dressed in boxers and a T-shirt. He looks clean-shaven and fresh. He smiles like he doesn't have a care in the world. Behind him is his bag, neatly packed.

"I couldn't leave without saying good-bye to you, Evan."

"I'm sorry—"

"Don't be. This racing business is all a gamble. I took a risk, and I lost."

Just like that, he admits fault. Deep down I had a shred of hope he would offer an explanation I could believe.

"I just want you to know what a great teammate you've been. I know you have big plans for college to become a hot-shit doctor and all, but it's just too bad you can't stick with the bike. If I had your legs at eighteen, I would've won seven Tours de France by now."

This should be the greatest compliment of my life, but I can barely hear it over the scream inside my head: *Cheater, cheater, cheater.* Before I can reply, there's the sound of a key card being swiped at the door, and Bernard, dressed to ride, enters the room. So if he's not in the shower, who is?

"Hell, I'm black-and-blue trying to get through that pack of media wolves in the lobby," says Bernard. "They want a pound of your flesh. You got your story down?"

"Think so. How's this?" Dash goes through his interview routine: a look in the distance, a sucking-in of breath, a slight cock of the head, and then the sincere look straight into the camera. "I discovered some blood in my stool, and my doctor prescribed a medication to stop the internal bleeding, and that caused the positive drug test. I was warned racing with only one kidney was dangerous, but it's not worth dying for."

Bernard laughs. "Is that even biologically feasible?"

"Beats the hell out of me. Ask Doogie Howser, MD."

They both look at me. Reluctantly, I nod. They burst out laughing.

"That's pretty good," says Bernard. "There will be an investigation, though."

"Who the hell cares? Today I'll be all over the media, and tomorrow it will be some other poor sucker and I'll be old news."

"Articles will be written," says Bernard.

"Don't be silly. No one *reads* anymore. I'll get slapped with a six-month to one-year suspension and be back before you know it."

I realize the water has stopped running. Kristee emerges from the bathroom wearing only a towel, which explains why she never met me yesterday. It's plain that Dash cheats at more than cycling. No one greets her, nor does she look our way as she gathers her clothes and retreats back into the bathroom. I actually thought she cared about me.

"What will you do?" asks Bernard.

"There's plenty to do." Dash pauses as if he's thinking. "Pour a little concrete in the backyard."

"And?"

He shrugs. "See Europe?"

They laugh harder. Everything is a big joke with these guys. Kristee, now dressed, emerges from the bathroom.

"Seriously," says Dash, "it will be a chance for me to spend some quality time with the wife and kids."

I glance over at Kristee, who doesn't even flinch as she faces the mirror, combing her hair with her fingers. Why did he have to say that in front of her?

Dash's phone rings, and he checks the ID. "It's Suzie." He answers the call with "Hi, Princess." There's a pause as he listens to her talk. "Haven't faced the media circus yet. I'm barricaded here in my hotel room with a couple of teammates trying to come up with a good story. I think we've got one." He listens some more, and sighs. "It's a risk we took, Princess, and we got busted. You know they weren't able to detect it last year. Those drug tests are getting smarter."

As Kristee passes Dash on the way out, her fingertips trail over his shoulder and down his arm, but he doesn't even look her way, as if he can't see or feel her.

"Hi, Evan." A weak smile flickers on her lips, then fades.

There's so much I want to say to her, but not now, not in front of Bernard and Dash. I can't even come up with a simple hi, but just stand there staring back at her. She throws back her shoulders, lifts her chin, and sashays out the door.

Dash gets off the phone. "My turn," he says, and heads for the shower.

Bernard opens a newspaper like it's just an ordinary morning. Facing me is the headline: DASH DOPES.

I bolt for the door and sprint down the hall. "Kristee," I yell after her.

Her shoulders rise to her ears as if she's been hit from behind. She hesitates a moment, then walks faster, but in her heels she's easy to catch.

I grab her shoulder and spin her around. "What were you doing back there?"

"What did it look like?"

"He was just using you."

"You don't know what's between Dash and me."

"Why'd you try to start something with me?"

She shrugs, lowers her lashes, then looks straight into my face. "Why not?"

My stomach churns like a pinwheel. "You acted so into me. Or were you just using me to get your *stories*?"

"Oh, grow up, little boy. If you're going to be in a man's race, act like a man. People use each other. The other night you needed a shoulder to cry on, so you used me for that."

Shame flushes my face. "I never . . . You don't care who you hurt!"

"I *hurt* you? Oh, please!"

"Dash is married."

"And you're in love with another girl."

"We broke up." I look away, then back at her. "And you're a home wrecker."

"Who are you to judge me, Evan? You think I'm the only girl Dash goes with?"

"Kristee . . ."

"What?"

I don't know what. I stare at her with pleading eyes, and she glares back, a fiery anger in her black pupils. I don't know how much time passes before she whirls around, her damp hair grazing my cheek. This time I don't go after her.

There's nothing to do but get ready to ride, but when I reach my room, I sink to the foot of the bed and sit there staring at the carpet. I don't want to ride. I don't want to go home. I don't want to move.

Some time later I hear a rap on the door and Bernard calling me. I let him in and return to my spot. He plops down on the bed next to me.

"You riding today?" he asks.

I shrug. "I don't see much point to it."

"We could use you."

"I thought you didn't want me on the team."

Just when I think Bernard is finally giving me some credit, he adds, "With two riders down, you're better than nothing."

"Gee, thanks."

He whacks my shoulder with his cycling cap and laughs.

"Does Mike know Dash took drugs?"

"He does now."

"Rainier—did he know?"

"I'm guessing Dash acted alone. Guys at the top are desperate to win."

"There's winners who don't cheat."

"There's winners who don't get caught."

"The hell!" I slap my thighs. "Not everyone dopes!"

"One year a certain substance is on the banned list,

another year it's some other thing. You take an aspirin or a NO-DOZ, you're taking a drug."

I know Greg LeMond was once suspected of doping for taking iron supplements when returning to racing after he nearly died in a hunting accident. Even the great Eddy Merckx was busted for a prescribed cough syrup. All of this seems petty, and yet the dangers are real. When Tommy Simpson collapsed and died of exhaustion while climbing Mont Ventoux in the 1967 Tour de France, amphetamines were found in his pocket.

"You know what the great Coppi said when he was asked if he used drugs?" asks Bernard. "'Only on the days I need them.'"

"Does Dash's wife know he cheats on her?"

"Suzie knows when to look the other way. She doesn't think divorce is especially good for kids, and she accepts that Dash isn't perfect. This way of making a living is hard on family life. Guys get lonely. Wives, too. Both of mine found someone else."

"Both?"

"Yeah. Twiced divorced. Got a couple of kids getting raised by their stepdads."

"Do you dope?" I ask bluntly.

He shakes his big head. "I'm not the type of guy that gets away with stuff. There, happy?" He stands and ruffles my hair like I'm a little kid. "Bus leaves in ten minutes. You gonna be on it, Sunny Boy?"

Finally, it's sunny, 68 degrees, fine riding weather here in downtown Visalia. It seems like a nice town, with a clock tower and murals of orange groves and the Sierra Nevada. Thousands of fans crowd the streets, but it's hard to share their enthusiasm. It's our longest stage, 134 miles, and nothing but flats the first 100 miles, before a few rolling hills into Paso Robles. In a team meeting the previous evening, Mike told us we were now riding for Sal. He's a good climber, but the hard climbing is over. A champion is good at everything. Waiting at the start, our six-man team looks to be no match for Klaus Grunwald, who didn't lose the yellow jersey after all. Temir Laptev, last year's champion, is only seconds down on him.

After our usual parade around downtown, we head southwest. As we pass the College of the Sequoias, a driver in a white lift truck gets impatient. He peels out in front of the entourage causing the lead motorcycles to brake and riders in the peloton to jostle against each other. A cop puts on his lights and siren and chases the guy down.

The streets beneath our wheels are chalked with Dash's name. Down Tulare Avenue we pass two convalescent homes, the residents lined up on the sidewalks in wheelchairs holding a long, hand-painted stretch of butcher paper reading Go, Dash, Go. We turn south and pass a high school where students are lined up at the fence, some of them bearing signs: Dash, Dash, Dash! No one, it seems, has gotten the memo that our star rider got busted.

Beyond the outskirts of town, there's nothing but flat land. The brown fields are plowed in diagonal rows that shoot to the horizon. I hate the flats, can't get comfortable on the bike with gravity pressing down on my feet, hands, and ass. An annoying crosswind blows from the northwest.

I miss Dash. Without Dash there's just no reason to ride. I want to abandon, but the Tour of California seems like a habit I can't quit. I wonder what Klaus thinks about Dash's doping, but he doesn't mention him when we're in earshot.

A group of six riders attack, forming an echelon, a paceline spread diagonally across the road, each man riding slightly to the left of the rider before him rather than directly behind him, gaining shelter against the crosswind. The breakaway gains a gap of thirty seconds, then two minutes, then five. Nobody chases; nobody cares. Our job is merely to keep Sal neck and neck with Klaus and Temir. We know it would be a waste of energy to try to break away from such powerful riders on flat land.

By late morning the temperature warms to 72 degrees and feels great. Nobody wants to work today. The pace is more like a club ride, as the riders talk and joke together in the sunshine. It might even be fun if Dash were here to liven up the conversation. We zigzag southwest through the countryside, passing through Guernsey, the outskirts of Corcoran, and Helm Corner. We pass dairies and vineyards, walnut orchards, and more and more cultivated land, filled with nothing.

At mile 87 we turn onto Highway 46, heading north to Paso Robles. We've allowed the breakaway to run up a six-minute gap when Taraz decides to reel them in. Temir's domestiques push the pace. No more Sunday ride. The gap begins to diminish, down to five minutes, then three and a half, then two. At last, there's a few rolling hills to climb, a chance to lift my sorry ass out of the saddle. With twenty miles to go, the exhausted, hardworking breakaway, which has been toiling against the wind for over four hours, is caught like scared rabbits by a pack of hounds.

It's clear that no one will escape today, and the finish is going to be one massive bunch sprint in which one man will win the stage and a three-second time bonus, while all the other riders in the peloton will receive the same time.

As we pass under the one-kilometer-to-go arch the sprinters and their lead-out men move forward and jostle for position. Temir, hungry for a stage win, is contesting the sprint front center. Tension is high in the pack, elbows knocking elbows, shoulders pressed to shoulders. This is my first pro bunch-sprint finish, and it's hairy.

Temir attacks, whips around his lead-out man, and moves his front wheel decisively ahead of Kronen's sprinter as he crosses the line. Temir controls his bike with one hand as he straightens one arm before him, fist clenched as if he holds the win in his palm.

He doesn't. Far to the right, out of his peripheral vision, our man Charles Larocque was first, capturing Stage 6 of the Tour of California in a stunning upset. After some tense moments of race officials deliberating over the photo finish, Charles rises to the podium. It makes my heart glad to see the Image Craft–Icon jersey center stage just one day after Dash has been barred. Kristee and the blond podium girl kiss Charles's cheeks and hand him a bouquet and the California bear.

Klaus Grunwald is awarded a fresh yellow jersey, and the GC standings remain the same. Sal is still in red for King of the Mountains. Charles doesn't have enough sprinters' points to wear green, but it's all good. He won the stage! After reporters swarm him and depart, I see him talking and laughing with Kristee. I'm sure it's just a friendly chat. Charles really is a confirmed family man with eight-year-old twin daughters he's always bragging about.

I overhear the conversation of two newscasters from a cable TV sports network. "Look at Larocque chatting it up with that podium girl," the short, bald one says to his colleague. "I barely got two words out of him."

"Yeah?" says the other guy, who is taller and paunchy. "Well, she's easier on the eyes than you are."

I've had 134 rather boring miles to mull over what went down between Kristee and me, and I've decided at least I owe her a recommendation. "She's good," I say, butting into the TV guys' conversation. "She wants to break into commentating."

"Oh, hello, Evan," says the bald guy. "Congratulations again on that awesome Stage Three win."

I'm still not used to people I don't know calling me by name. "Thanks, but that was given to me."

"By the doper?" the paunchy man says.

"By Dashiell Shipley," I say, giving them a steely-eyed glare, which they don't argue with. "As for Kristee, you should really give her a try. She knows a lot about cycling, even raced herself, and she's got experience as a weather girl."

"Where do you know her from?" asks the bald man, his tone weighed with innuendo.

"Stage Three, on the podium," I reply honestly. "Where else am I gonna meet a podium girl?"

"Well, we do have an internship program," says the taller one, still watching Charles and Kristee talking together. "Not much pay, but—"

"She'd be grateful for the chance! You guys could be known as the network with the girl cycling commentator. You'd get more viewers, I bet. Come on, I'll introduce you."

During the short ride down the coast I doze off, but the bus coming to a halt in front of our motel jolts me awake. I look out the window and see a windmill. In this area everywhere you look there's a windmill.

I yawn and stretch and go sit next to our mechanic, George. I begin making arrangements with him to take out my time trial bike early tomorrow morning to ride the course.

"You can't do that," says Bernard. "They'll be hundreds of fans riding the course before the race tomorrow."

"No worries, Evan," says George. "I'll drive you over it."

"It's not the same," I say.

"It's not like you have to actually race it," says Bernard.

"I want to."

Bernard looks at Rainier, who looks at Mike, who nods his head. "That's the spirit, Evan. I'd like to see what you can really do in a time trial."

"So I'll ride the course right now," I say, rising to my feet and rubbing my sore quads.

Bernard groans. "Five hours in the saddle isn't enough for our Sunny Boy. Do you even know the way?"

I've studied it in the course book so many times, I think I've got it memorized, but after 134 miles of riding my mind is a bit fuzzy. "Sort of."

"Hell, I'll go with you," says Bernard.

I had imagined some time alone, a nice, leisurely spin, but with Bernard nothing is ever leisurely or nice. With Dash and Armand both out of the race, we have become roommates for the first time tonight, something else I'm not thrilled about. "No, Bernard, really. You don't have to—"

He holds up his palm. "Better wait dinner for us, Mike."

"Dinner's on me," says Charles. "I know the perfect place."

Bernard and I ride out to the Solvang Time Trial course, past the ostrich farm, with George driving support in the team car. First thing, Bernard starts picking apart the way I'm sitting on the bike.

"Farther forward. Farther! Shoulders behind elbow pads. That's it. Hide your knees from the wind. Flat back. Flatter!"

As I make each adjustment I feel myself and the bike flowing together, not like my experience in Sacramento, when it seemed like I was fighting it. At first there's some short steep climbs, which we go over a couple of times, trying to select the best gear.

"You can push it a little on these climbs, but don't overcook it," says Bernard. "It's always better to start easy and build up to a faster pace."

We go over and over a number of turns, searching for the smoothest pavement and any chance of a slight decline. Cornering is a big part of time trialing. I know if I take turns too slowly, I'll lose time; take them too fast, and I'll be bodysurfing on asphalt.

"Concentrate on shaving off seconds," says Bernard. "Those add up to minutes eventually. If you don't think you're working hard enough, increase the rpms rather than going up a gear, but don't be afraid of a bigger gear if you need it."

We ride through Ballard and onto sweeping Roblar Avenue, leading toward Los Olivos. At the flagpole we turn left and head toward the ascent.

"It's easier than it looks," say Bernard, "so don't get excited like you're actually tackling Bonny Doon."

This takes me back to leading Dash into Santa Cruz, my greatest moment in the TOC.

"The son of a bitch," says Bernard, as if he can read my mind. "He didn't need that crap to be great. I tried to tell him."

"It was hard without him today. I lacked purpose and kept wondering why I was still riding."

"Sunny boy! I thought you ride to finish!"

I have to smile. Was I once so naive? Could I have changed so much in just a few days of racing?

"What you said, you said just right. I lacked purpose, too," admits Bernard. "But we've got purpose now. Smoking ole Klaus and Temir tomorrow! I'm glad you dragged me out here. Me and Dash went over this course dozens of times this winter, but a quick review is just what I needed."

We scramble up the incline overlooking neat rows of vines

on the hillside. Bernard barrels down Ballard Canyon and waits for me at the bottom. Tapping his watch, he says "You drop like a grandma. Let's try it again."

We help George load the bikes on the car's roof rack and drive back up to the top of the canyon. Bernard is a little more satisfied with my second descent, and after the third it's too dark to see the road.

As we load the bikes I see a guy about my age with a backpack on, riding his bike, probably on his way home from school after a late practice. How long has it been since I was just a regular high-school kid? Years, it seems. No, wait a minute, I still am. The thought unnerves me.

Bernard bumps my elbow, which makes me realize I've been staring at the guy coasting out of sight in the dusk.

"What's the matter, Sunny? You look like you've seen a ghost."

When our team steps into Los Olivos Cafe, I look down the whole wall of wine. "Damn! Too bad Armand abandoned. He would love this place."

"Armand was a wine connoisseur?" asks Charles, taking out a handwritten list of wines and setting wire-rimmed glasses on his nose. "Too bad I didn't know."

"I think he was a wine hater," I say. "California wines, anyway."

"He couldn't have hated them all," says Bernard.

The hostess leads us to a long table prepared for us. Charles immediately orders several bottles of wine from his list and Calistoga sparkling water for me. The menu is filled with awesome things to eat, and I wish I could order one of each. I decide on braised beef on brioche for an appetizer, lasagna with spinach and ground turkey, and chocolate pizza for dessert. When the food arrives, it looks beautiful on the plate and smells mouth-drooling delicious. I try not to gobble it down without tasting it.

"This would be a damn fine tour if it were held in May," says Bernard.

"It couldn't be in May," says Sal. "The Giro is in May. This isn't bad weather. Have you ever ridden Paris-Nice?" he asks.

"Oh, yeah. Always ugly weather there," agrees Bernard. "The crosswind blows so hard, it seems like the rain is falling sideways."

"The worse the weather, the better for me," brags Sal. "This rider quits, that rider quits, I ride, I ride."

The team is in high spirits, their voices rising louder and louder as they take turns telling war stories. Bernard, Sal, and Charles have ridden the three week-long grand tours: the Tour de France, the *Giro d'Italia,* and *Vuelta a España.*

Sal recalls growing up in San Remo and painting the streets with the names of his cycling heroes, Claudio Chiappucci and Marco Pantani, to welcome the *Giro* passing through his town. "Even as a small boy, I want to be a racer," says Sal, his weathered brown face bright with the wine and tomato sauce stuck in the creases of his mouth. Charles talks about his favorite classics, the prestigious one-day road races in Europe. In a stage race a sprinter can only hope to win an individual stage, but in the classics, he's able to win the whole thing. Charles reenacts winning the Belgium race Liège-Bastogne-Liège in a chaotic bunch sprint. Bernard tells about one Tour de France in which he lead Dash up the Alps in a snowstorm, and on the descent one rider missed a hairpin turn, flew off the side of the mountain, and survived only because he landed on snow rather than rocks.

I eat and listen. Their stories are too awesome, the food is too delicious, the restaurant is too warm and bright and loud, as if my senses are on fire. I am a pro bike racer sitting down with my pro bike team.

Bernard knocks my shoulder with his. "You're awful quiet, sunny."

"I don't have any stories to tell."

"But you do," says Charles, saluting me with his wineglass. "You managed to hang in with the peloton for one hundred thirty-four long miles on Stage Six of the Tour of California to see the great Charles Larocque take the win in a dazzling bunch sprint."

I laugh along with the guys because the story is really about him.

"And on Stage Three of the Tour of California up the climb of Tunitas Creek, you dropped the great Salvatore Netti and went on to become King of the Mountains!" says Sal, raising his glass to me.

"And on that same stage of the Tour of California," says Mike, "you paced the great Dashiell Shipley up the notorious Bonny Doon grade, and upon arriving in Santa Cruz, you captured the stage!"

"And when you were discovered at a Phoenix winter training camp," says Bernard, "the great Bernard Nagle insisted you were a scrawny, inexperienced kid who couldn't possibly pull his weight in the Tour of California, but you proved him wrong and went on to become the great Evan Boroughs."

My teammates' cheers and hoots roar in my ears as my vision blurs.

"Uh, would you excuse me?" I make a run for it, unable to bear them seeing tears in my eyes. In the narrow, dark hall, I withdraw my phone from my pocket.

"Glory?"

"Yes."

"Oh, Glory, Glory, Glory."

"What's up, Evan?"

"I just like saying your name. I miss you so much. I feel strange, Glory. I feel . . . not me." She is quiet, waiting for me to go on. "You know *The Lion, the Witch and the Wardrobe*? How the kids had to pass through a . . . like a . . . shit!"

"Portal," she prompts.

"Right! I feel like I'm about to pass through a portal and . . . It's just weird, and I feel a little crazy."

"Well, probably the first day back will be hard. Getting out of bed will be the biggest challenge. Then you'll go to school and period one will pass, and then period two and three, then lunch—"

"We have lunch after fourth."

"Fourth, then. You'll call me at lunch, right? To tell me how it's going. And you'll say, 'It's going. It's not as bad as I thought.' And I'll say, 'I knew it wouldn't be.' By the end of the day, it will be back to same-old."

"I think it will take the whole week."

"Okay, the whole week."

"Glory? You'll take me back, won't you? You can be friends with Alfred. I don't mind. He can come on all our dates, but he can't sit between us."

She laughs. "Why don't you finish the race before we try to figure things out?"

"I love you, Glory."

"I'll always love you, too, Evan, but . . ."

"But?"

"I'm not so sure anymore that we're right for each other."

"Ah, Glory—"

"We'll talk when you get home. Be safe, Evan. Ride fast."

Chapter Fourteen

Stage 7: Solvang Time Trial, 15 Miles

The night before the Solvang Time Trial, I am either awake visualizing every turn, slope, and rough patch on the course or I am dreaming it. Bernard must be doing the same thing because around two A.M. his light wakes me up, and I find him bent over the course book, tracing the route with his finger.

"I'm setting my goals high," he says in the morning as we get ready. "I want to break thirty minutes." No one has ever done this.

"I want to break thirty-four."

"You'll do it," he says. "You know why the time trial is called the race of truth."

I nod. It truly reveals how good a rider is. With no domestiques bucking the wind and spilling their guts, a rider is out there alone, proving his mettle.

"We're going to kick ass." Bernard clamps my shoulder in emphasis.

Long, long ago, six days to be exact, I was ranked 128th, and therefore the first rider to start the Sacramento Time Trial. Today is different. For one thing, only 103 riders remain, and of those I'm ranked eighteenth. Bernard is fourth, Sal is third, and Temir is second. Since Klaus is the World Time Trial Champion, it's predicted that he'll hold on to the yellow jersey today.

As Bernard suspected, in the hours before the start, the course is swarming with fans on their bicycles. It's a perfect, clear morning to ride, in the low sixties. The first rider is off at noon. Warming up on the trainer, I have a nice view of the town, with its steeply pitched green and pink roofs, decorative windmills, and fluttering red-and-white Danish flags.

Each minute another rider shoots out of the yellow start house. When it's close to my turn, I'm more excited than nervous.

Rainier waits with me. "How do you feel?"

"Great, really great."

"What's your target?"

"A thirty-four. I think I can do at least a thirty-four."

"Of course you can. Conditions are perfect, tailwind on the upside. What are your challenges? The descent, perhaps?"

"Naw, Bernard helped me with that. It's focus. My mind tends to wander when I ride, and I've got to maintain concentration."

"Very good. Check your power meter and miles per hour. Riders think pushing a bigger gear is the way to win in a shorter race, but that's not always true. See if you can increase your watts with a faster cadence. You're up, Evan. Good luck."

"Thanks, Rainier. Thanks for everything." I begin to mount

the steps to the start house, and he stops me with his hand on my shoulder. "About that thirty-four, I think you'll surprise yourself."

Soon I'm on the bike, clipped into the pedals. The starter's assistant is holding me upright as I shift around on the seat trying to find the best position. I hear the crowd's muffled roar from outside the start house. I take deep breaths, and all my nerve endings seem to tingle in anticipation. The starter begins his countdown. I watch his splayed hand before me. Five fingers, then four, three, two, one. I rise up and stomp on my pedals. Out of the shoot I soar, down the ramp, the fans chanting, "Evan! Evan! Evan!" My lead motorcycle speeds ahead of me, while Pablo drives a team car behind me.

I blast down Main Street and hang a left. It's a good thing Bernard and I went over and over this section because I'm faced with two short, steep climbs, when all day the commentator has called the course flat. I maneuver through several corners, remembering the fastest, cleanest route through each one.

My ride is going great, and by the time I'm whipping through Ballard, I can see my minute man, a tiny, black fly speck in the distance. Am I going too fast too soon? Will I blow up on the second half? I don't think so; I feel too good now. The black dot ahead of me becomes larger. It grows distinctive features: a body, a head. I can distinguish colors: the white, blue, and orange of a Rabobank rider. It would be awesome to catch and pass my minute man.

I'm on the sweeping curve of Roblar Avenue, the wind shifting as my direction changes. Fans have come out of their houses to cheer as the racers pass. Nearing Los Olivos, I see my minute man has grown legs and a helmet. A timer shouts out my halfway time: 20:06. It's a bit disappointing, but I know the second half of the course is much swifter than the first.

I enter Los Olivos, greeted by many more fans, sight the

Los Olivos Cafe, where we had our team dinner, turn left, and head out of town toward the climb. My minute man is in full view now, a switchback above me. I'm going to catch him! I rise out of my saddle and attack and attack and—*there!*—I got him! I crest the peak, thinking it would be humiliating if he caught me on the descent.

Another rider up ahead! I'm gonna pass *two* minute men? Oh, but this AirCom rider is in deep trouble. He's flatted, and without his team car nearby, he's continuing to ride. This is dangerous on a descent, where it's easy to roll a tire. Too bad for him, but yea for me. I've passed my second minute man. I'm having a spectacular ride, but I know that could change any second. I grip the aerobars tighter and think positive.

After the descent there are a few rolling hills, but nothing big. I'm back on Main Street, and it's all over so soon. I check my stopwatch on the bars: unofficial time—32.44!

Pablo is there to take my bike. "Great ride, Evan."

"Thanks."

"Yes, good job, man." Max hands me my warm-ups, shoes, and a recovery drink.

Now I get to rest and watch the other riders come in. Finally, it's Sal's turn to finish. I look down the road in anticipation, and spot the blue-and-red of Image Craft–Icon. It's not Sal but Bernard who thunders across the line, huffing and puffing like an angry bull. He's looking strong, but where's Sal?

"He's done it!" the announcer shouts. "Bernard Nagle finishes at 29:56, the new best time and a course record!"

Sal sprints across the line, his minute man, Temir, close behind him. Bad news for Sal. Bad news for Image Craft–Icon. Sal brakes, and still straddling the bike, he whisks off his sunglasses, presses his forefinger and thumb into his eyes, and cries like a child. He has lost nearly a minute on the leaders.

As Klaus crosses the finish line, he shoots upright on his

saddle, extends both arms over his head, and holds up his forefinger to indicate he's number one. He's not. Temir Laptev has won the stage in the time of 29:50, and Klaus, the World Time Trial Champion is third, 11 seconds down.

The announcer rings out the news, "Temir Laptev, Tour of California's reigning champion, takes the yellow jersey for the first time this year!"

"Good for him," says Bernard, standing next to me. "I'd rather lose to him than that arrogant Sauerkraut."

I'm reminded that Bernard, as an ex-member of Kronen, was made to work for Klaus as well as Dash. "Maybe you won't lose to either one," I say.

Bernard looks at me hard. In his beady, nearly black eyes I see a spark of gratitude. "Sal is still fifteen seconds ahead of me. I guess that's who we'll be riding for tomorrow."

"You're the stronger rider. You proved it today."

He nods. "That's what I think. But what do Mike and Rainier think?"

His question hangs in the air as he makes his way to the stage to stand on the second-place block.

I duck out of the podium ceremony in quest of some of Solvang's famous cheese Danish. I'm two steps from the bakery, my mouth watering, when I see a college-age girl heading my way who reminds me of Meredith. She's heavier, though, in skintight jeans. Her long brown hair, parted down the middle, is greasy, and her face is raging with eruptions of acne that have been picked and scrubbed raw. It's true Meredith overeats when she's stressed and her skin breaks out, but unlike this girl, she always takes care of her appearance. The grin that stretches into a sneer I do recognize.

"Meredith!"

"Surprise!"

Our hug is brief and stiff as usual.

"How'd you get here? Are Mom and Dad here, too?"

"No, Santa Barbara is only forty-five minutes away."

"Oh, yeah, huh. I didn't think—"

"I didn't expect you to. Anyway, I thought I'd drive up. See what all the hoopla is about. How'd you do?"

"Good. I was going for a thirty-four and got a thirty-two."

"And that means?"

"Minutes."

"I still don't get it. All morning I've watched one guy after another pop out of that little yellow house and ride off alone. Obviously, the first guy is going to be hours ahead of the last guy."

I laugh. "It's called a time trial."

"It's boring. What are all these idiots standing around gawking at?" She sits on the edge of a flower box and removes cigarettes and a lighter from the pouch of her UCSB hoodie and lights up.

"Meredith!" My sister—a smoker? Is this some sort of joke?

She turns her head to exhale a puff of smoke, then meets my eyes defiantly. "What? I've got to do something to stop stuffing myself." She slaps her thighs. "These are my biggest jeans, and I'm such a whale, I'm about to rip out the seams."

"Oh, Mer, you are not."

"I'm failing," she says matter-of-factly.

My heart starts to pulse faster, but I keep my cool. "What does that mean? You got a B on a test?"

"No, Ren. It means I've got a C minus in calculus and a D minus in chemistry."

"You can get a tutor. You can study harder."

She puffs on her cigarette. "Been there, done that. It's the story of my life. Every time I got a low grade, I thought, I'll study harder. I'll try harder. I've wheedled grades from teachers, begged and badgered them, but that doesn't work anymore.

Wait till you get to college. You'll see. It's way harder than high school. Oh, but maybe not for you. Maybe you'll just coast through, like everything else."

"I don't coast."

"I studied my butt off for the SATs and what happened? You got a higher score without cracking the prep book."

"I studied. I—"

She waves her cigarette around. "Even *this* comes naturally for you, doesn't it?" She glares at me through puffy eyes, which are now welling up. "I've got good reason to hate you." She lowers her head and sobs, the tears dripping through her fingers and making dark spots on her jeans.

All during my childhood when Meredith was upset or unhappy, I somehow felt guilty, like it was my fault. I really don't need this right now. "I'm sorry you're having trouble in school."

"Sorry? What the hell good is that? I'll never be a doctor."

Always she's pretended to be so high-and-mighty, when in fact she's been afraid she's not good enough. Now I understand all those lame excuses our parents used to give me for letting Meredith have her way. What they were really trying to say is she just doesn't have as much to work with as I do. How can I fix this? "Uh, maybe you could be a physical therapist or a . . . a nurse."

"Our *parents* are nurses. All parents dream their kids will be something better than them. I won't be. I'm their failure." She glares at me through narrowed eyes. "It's up to you now."

I don't know what to say. All I can think of is escape. I try to think of excuses to get away from her: my team bus is leaving, or it's time for my massage. "Let's go get some cheese Danish."

She sniffles and looks hopeful. "I'd rather have ice cream."

I sigh inwardly. Meredith is used to getting what she wants. "Okay, then, ice cream."

"I'm too fat for ice cream."

"Naw, haven't you heard of the ice cream diet? For every scoop you eat, you lose a pound, except for Jamoca almond fudge. For that, it's two pounds."

"Oh, Ren, look at me. How will I ever lose all this weight?"

"You will. When you're ready to, you will."

She nods her agreement. She doesn't seem to notice I'm parroting our mom, who answers Meredith exactly the same way every time she asks her the same question over and over. It's sound advice. Since she's hit puberty, I've watched Meredith go to pieces and pull herself together a dozen times.

In the ice-cream shop, between licks of her double-scoop cone, Meredith says, "I'm surprised you're still in this race. Weren't you supposed to be riding for what's-his-face who got busted for drugs?"

"Yeah, but our team manager asked me to stay on. It sucks, though. I can't help taking this personally. It's like Dash cheated *me*."

"Poor Ren. Lost his boyhood hero. You were like ten when you put that guy's poster up on your wall."

"Fourteen, but still. He gave his kid a kidney. He gave me a stage win. But he's a cheat! He's not good to his wife, and then he treats Kristee, the podium girl, like she's nothing."

"The who?"

"Do you think it's possible—"

"That he needed those drugs? That he didn't really cheat?"

"No. Do you think it's possible to win without cheating?"

"I guess cheating does improve your odds."

"Mer!"

She laughs. "All right, then, cheaters never prosper. Is that what you want to hear? Mom taught us that during our kitchen table Monopoly games when you used to sneak money and hide it under the board."

"I never cheated at Monopoly; you were the one. When you were banker and handing out money, you used to hide five-hundred-dollar bills between your tens."

She points her finger at me. "No, you—"

"I'm not talking about kid games. I'm talking about pro cycling!"

She shrugs. "I don't see the difference."

"Me neither." Doping is cheating, and I'm not going to do it. If I lose, I lose. I think of Bernard's warning, how the pressures of professional sports causes a guy to give in to it. Not me, not ever.

"Hey, I heard Glory got accepted into Harvard! I bet that changes her plan of trotting off to UA with you in the fall."

"Glory . . . Glory and I broke up."

"For reals? When did this happen?"

"A couple of days ago, but we talked last night. I'm hoping she'll take me back."

"Hmm." Meredith thoughtfully swirls her tongue all the way around her cone. Obviously, the ice cream has improved her mood. "Glory and I got pretty chummy over winter break. The way she talked about you, I didn't even recognize you as my brother. She was crazy for you."

"Yeah?"

"Uh-huh. But maybe you don't look so good to her anymore with UA your only prospect. You should have applied to more colleges, Ren."

"I've been thinking . . ." I pause. I haven't said this to anyone. Why should I pick Meredith, my lifelong rival? But I'm feeling kind of close to her, and with the stress of the race, my

168

defenses are down. "I'm thinking I might not start college in the fall."

"Ren! Are you out of your mind? Why?"

My throat closes over, so I have to gulp to even swallow ice cream. "For this," I whisper. "For bike racing."

"Oh, no. Think again. You do that and you can kiss Glory good-bye for good, bike bum." She smiles so brightly, it almost makes her pretty. "Then I wouldn't feel so alone. We can be losers together."

That night the team assembles in a small conference room in our Thousand Oaks hotel to discuss strategies for the final stage. We're seated around an oval table while Rainier stands before us. As he describes the course he marks up a map of it, which is projected on the screen behind him, by an Elmo document camera. The Stage 8 Thousand Oaks/Westlake Village/ Agoura Hills circuit course is 20.6 miles, and we will ride four laps. Although there's a total of 7,200 feet of climbing, the ascent each lap is only 1,800 feet.

"We all know it wasn't Sal's day," says Rainier. "But he's only thirty-two seconds down. He can still win."

"Damn right he can," Mike interjects, "with the support of the greatest team here at the Tour of California!"

That's our cue to offer some enthusiasm, but we make no response. Thirty-two seconds is a lot. If the announcement upsets Bernard, he doesn't show it. Sal's brown, rubbery face breaks into an apologetic smile. At dinner he was unusually quiet, not cracking a single joke. I picture him at his finish today, hunched over the bars, sobbing.

"Your best chance, Sal, is to attack when they least expect it," says Rainier. "First lap would be best, but by the second lap you've go to act."

Bernard straightens in his chair, the color seeping into his face. "I thought on the fourth climb—"

"That's too late," Mike interrupts sternly. "That's what Klaus and Temir expect we'll do. And each one of you guys is going to bust your balls trying to get Sal launched on a breakaway. You're all domestiques tomorrow, got that?"

We all nod or say yes.

Mike claps his hands together. "That's it, then."

"I think we should ride for Bernard," I blurt.

Mike tugs on his beard and gives me a wary look.

"I mean, I know he's fifteen seconds down on Sal, but it's clear Bernard's been getting stronger every day, and he's an all-rounder and—"

Mike's eyebrows shoot up. Splotches of purple flood the pouches beneath his eyes. It's clear he's not taking this well, so I talk faster.

"Bernard can take long, hard pulls, and he can sprint, and he can descend like the devil, and Sal is a climbing specialist, and like, no offense to Sal, but there's not much to climb out there."

Rainier drops his eyes. Mike stares at me for what seems like a full minute, although it's probably only several seconds. Finally he speaks in a cold, steely tone, "Never mind the babbling of this ridiculous boy. Meeting is adjourned."

Everyone stands to leave.

"Stay put, Evan," says Mike.

When only he and I are left in the room, he shuts the door.

"I know you are of a younger generation that does not respect authority, but do you know what chain of command means?"

"Yes, sir," I say, my heart pounding.

"You don't have to pull the 'sir' shit on me, Evan," he says, his tone growing louder by the phrase. "I just need you to get one thing straight: I am the manager; you are the rider. I'm the general; you're the foot soldier. You play chess? You're a pawn; I'm the manager."

If he wanted to keep the analogy going, he should've said "king," but I'm smart enough not to point that out. I do respect authority, and I'm not used to getting yelled at.

"In this sport the managers move the little pawns around, and the little pawns do just as they're told and never talk back. Is that clear?"

"Yes, sir. I mean Mike."

"Bernard put you up to this?"

"Oh, no, s-s-s . . . Mike. It was just my opinion."

"Your opinion doesn't count. Now, I know you're just a kid having a week at the races, but you're on contract with my team. This is business, big business, and you just attacked the morale of my team. You just might have screwed up everything for us."

"I'm sorry."

"Sorry's no good. It doesn't help matters. Come with me. You're switching rooms with Joris."

I try to stand, but humiliation has left me immobile. Does he really think Bernard and I would conspire against him?

Chapter Fifteen

Stage 8: Thousand Oaks/Westlake Village/ Agoura Hills Circuit Race, 84 Miles

"Don't talk, just listen," says a guy over my cell, with an unknown caller ID. "Better yet, pretend it's your little girlfriend."

I don't explain the complication with Glory. I don't say anything. By now I recognize the voice: Dash Shipley. I look around the team's bus, which is transporting us to the start. Dedrick is in the seat ahead of me, bobbing his head to heavy metal blasting out of his iPod, Charles and Joris are at the table in front fueling up, and Sal and Bernard are bent over the course book with Rainier, discussing possible places to make a break. Mike is on the seat across from me scrolling through text on his phone. Occasionally he writes information down on a pocket-sized notebook he always carries. I don't know if he'd like me talking to Dash. I sure don't want to make him mad again.

"Say, Hey, Glory," Dash prompts me.

"Hey, Glory," I repeat.

"Very convincing. You sound like a zombie. I hear you got a good reaming from the head honcho last night." He laughs. "Good idea, wrong way to present it. Never at a team meeting, buckaroo. Never mind, you'll learn. Mike's a good guy, fighting for a light suspension for me. Probably I'll get it, too."

"But you . . ." I pause.

"Yeah, yeah, I know. You think I cheated. Let's agree to disagree on that. You'll see how it is if you keep at this. Anyhow, I'll be clean from now on. Can't afford another positive test. But enough about me; let's talk about you. I hope you know today's game plan is Mike's idea, not Rainier's. Even if Sal could get away on the second lap, which he can't, by the third lap he'd be dog food for a ravenous German shepherd I know. You're right. It's gotta be the fourth, on the climb, and it's gotta be Bernard. Now say, Oh, cool! I can't wait to see you, baby."

"Go on."

"You know how you won the third stage for me?"

Actually I won the third stage, but I know what he means. "Yeah."

"You're going to do the same for Bernard. Only instead of Bonny Doon, it's gonna be Mulholland. On the fourth lap you're going to bust a lung pulling Bernard up the climb and over the rollers before the descent. This will work. Bernard and I already talked."

"Yeah, but—"

"You know how to get in good with Mike again? Bring him home a winner. That'll be Bernard. The guy deserves it, all these years busting his ass as a domestique. Now it's

173

his turn to shine. Don't let him down. Now say, Bye, Glory. See you soon, babe." There's a beep-beep-beep of a disconnected call.

"Bye, Glory. See you soon, babe."

Mike puts away his phone and slides over to sit by me.

My nerve endings start to short out, just thinking of the tongue-lashing he gave me last night. Did he overhear Dash's voice on my phone?

"Feel good today?" he asks.

"Fine. Ready to go."

"Got a little more to give Image Craft–Icon?"

I nod, hoping I don't look guilty. "I'll give it everything I've got."

"I know you will, Evan. You've been a great asset to our team. I usually like my riders to take it one day at a time, focus on the job at hand, but I've decided to give you something else to think about. I know you came on board for a one-shot deal, but I'm hoping you'll want to continue riding with us." He rips the page out of his notebook that he's been working on and hands it to me. It reads: EVAN'S RACE PROGRAM. "This is just a rough draft."

"But I have to—"

"Finish high school, go to college. I know. This is designed to work around that. Look it over. We can talk later."

On the program are the Philadelphia International Championship, the Cascade Cycling Classic, and the U.S. Pro Road Championships, but even more exciting are some European races, such as Clásica San Sebastián, Paris-Brussels, and the Giro di Lombardia. "Wow, pro racing in Europe! You're really giving me this chance?"

"Just for the experience. It will be utterly grueling and damn discouraging, but you'll learn." He taps my quad with his notebook and rises from the seat. "Good luck today, Evan."

The Thousand Oaks/Westlake Village/Agoura Hills Circuit begins at a huge, fancy shopping mall called The Oaks. We're straddling our bikes at the start line, under clear skies, and I'm anxious to get going. There's a mass of people leaning over the yellow Tour of California barriers cheering and yelling. The announcer gets on the mike and starts thanking a bunch of corporate sponsors. After that, I'm sure we'll get the show on the road, but no, some hefty gal in a tube top and miniskirt has to sing "The Star-Spangled Banner." I'm really starting to hate that song. Every time I hear it, it's like the singers are in competition to see how many notes they can hit that aren't in the tune. I vote to have it swapped out for the "Battle Hymn of the Republic." Glory, Glory, Hallelujah!

As the singer croons on, the racers hold their helmets to their hearts. I hear a low, deep voice muttering, "Excuse me, 'cuse me, pardon." Bernard appears in my peripheral vision, knocking handlebars and elbows as he shoves into the position next to me, despite the disgruntled looks the Kronen riders give him.

"Did Dash get a hold of you?" he mutters.

"Yeah."

"What do you think?"

"What do you think?"

"I asked you first," he says.

I tilt my head toward the singer. "Do we have to talk about this *now*?"

"I think over cocktails this evening would be a little late."

"If I go against the plan, do you think it would make Mike unhappy with me?"

"It could."

I think of my lovely European race program ripped to pieces. I think how ecstatic everyone would be, including

Mike, if Bernard won the TOC for Image Craft–Icon. I think of Sartre saying, "We make ourselves."

"First, we'll try to do what Mike wants," says Bernard. "If we can get Sal launched in a breakaway—great. Ain't gonna happen, though."

I nod. "Fourth lap, last climb," I whisper.

The ends of Bernard's smile rise above his hooked nose. "Awesome. I knew I could count on you."

When the stage finally gets under way, we ride in a neutral zone down Thousand Oaks Boulevard. A few miles later, on Townsgate Road, we get the green light, and the peloton revs up on flat Agoura Road. We pass through Westlake Village and head to Agoura Hills. Charles and some of the other sprinters attack and gain a gap of about a hundred yards to jam for the first sprint points. Charles places second in the sprint, and the sprinters allow themselves to be absorbed back into the pack. After we turn onto Cornell Road, we hit some fairly easy rollers.

Temir, in the yellow jersey, looks relaxed and confident. All he has to do today is keep Klaus, Sal, and Bernard in sight. Klaus is probably wondering where he can gain nine seconds on Temir, not even thinking of Sal or Bernard as serious threats.

The peloton corners to begin the nine-mile stretch on Mulholland Highway. The riders bob up and down as they climb the short, steep, 900-foot ascent up Rock Store Mountain. Bernard surges ahead a little, and Klaus and Temir are right there with him. After reaching the Rock Store, the peloton ducks under an overhanging rock on a short descent, then begins the two-and-a-half-mile climb to the KOM. No one presses the pace; no one tries to get away. It's the first of four times up this thing, and we're all just testing it out.

Super Heckler Man jumps out from behind a rock waving his arms, his red cape flapping behind him, and begins jogging beside me, shouting, "Ev-an! Ev-an! Can't you go any faster?"

Damn, this guy again. I got a nice rest from him the past two days. I wonder if I can shift over to the other side of the road for the next ascent, but then maybe he'll anticipate my move and reappear there.

Temir and Klaus don't contest the KOM, and Sal wins it. If he doesn't win the whole race, at least he'll go home with the red jersey.

We glide over rolling hills of the Santa Monica Mountains wilderness. A few multimillion-dollar residences are situated along the roadside, and in the distance are rock formations, sagebrush, and oak woodlands. We turn on Westlake Boulevard and plunge down the twisty, technical descent. Klaus, Temir, and Bernard lead the way, but I take it cautiously, which causes me to drift back through the peloton. This is probably not so smart, because when we reach the floor of the Conejo Valley, the riders are packed tight, and I'm forced to knock handlebars and throw an occasional elbow, fighting my way through the pack.

When I get to the front, Bernard says, "Where'd you go? You scared me."

I don't answer, but merely promise myself I'll be more aggressive on the descents.

Putting on a show for the fans at the sprint zone, several riders get a little crazy and cause a minor pileup. It's a lucky distraction, and Sal, Bernard, Charles, and I manage to get away. Kronen and Taraz lead the peloton in a chase, and soon we're caught on Cornell Road.

"Good effort," says Mike over our radios, but even he,

by now, must realize how futile it is to try breaking away so soon.

At the base of Rock Store Mountain, Sal launches a surprise attack, and Bernard jumps on his wheel. They manage to stay away long enough to capture the KOM points, but they're caught on the rollers. During the third lap all three of us surge on the second long ascent, but we're caught again.

Mike's disgust is apparent in his tone. "Guys! Why don't you act like you mean it?"

It all comes down to the fourth lap. Starting the two-part climb, Sal drifts back in the peloton. Having sprinted up this sucker three times, he's clearly done. I feel Bernard pouring on the pressure, making the pace uncomfortable for a lot of riders. The peloton comes unglued, stringing over the ascent up Rock Store Mountain. On the flat part between climbs, I turn my head to try to spot some signal from Bernard. My heart is yammering more out of anxiety than physical exertion. When do we go? What if we fail? Why don't we do something?

"Boo!" someone yells into my ear, causing me to nearly fly off my bike and out of my skin. Super Heckler Man wiggles his fingers in my face and waggles his tongue.

"Damn it!" I growl through clenched teeth. "I've had enough of you!" I jump on my pedals and hammer like hell, pulling up on one side of the bars and then the other, rocking the bike fiercely up the mountain, my shoulders aching with the effort.

"Evan! Wait for me!" Bernard yells. He jumps on my wheel and away we go.

"Two bike lengths," Mike says in my ear. "Three, four. How about pouring on a little more, Evan?"

I'm already flat-out, but somehow I've got to give more. "What . . . what's happening?" I pant.

"Temir is falling back," says Mike excitedly. "Klaus is still chasing, but you're gaining ground. By god, you might have them!"

We crest the hill, then jam on the rollers. With our speeding over easy terrain and the leaders still stuck on the climb, our gap increases. Our team car is at our side, Mike sticking his hand out, thumb up. If I can just drag Bernard to the descent, he can bomb down it alone and time-trial the flats to the finish.

I'm fading, though. My right lower back feels as if a monster has grabbed a fist full of my muscles and is twisting them like rope. Lactic acid burns through my legs. I clench my teeth and fight for one more powerful turn of the cranks and then another. Hang on! Bernard needs me. I can ride through the pain if I will it. We make ourselves. *We make ourselves.* My pulse roars in my ears; my grunts erupt like cries.

I think my job is nearly done, but then Bernard yells breathlessly, "Don't die on me now, damn you. I'll need a tow on the flats." He pounds the pedals and rockets by, his sweat spraying me. Gulping air, I tuck in behind him.

Down, down we plunge. How am I supposed to keep up with Bernard on this wicked descent? Hell, I'll wipe out trying. I've never gone this fast, and still his wheel is speeding away. I lean far over the front of my bike to catch up. Then it happens: I slip into the zone. I have always dreaded descents in races, but this one is pure joy. As I whiz down the canyon every adjustment to steering, every shift of my weight is just right. My head is clear and my breathing steady. Bernard streaks ahead of me, but as soon as it's flat enough to turn the cranks, I catch him.

We trade pace frequently, taking short, hard pulls, Bernard's stronger than mine. Eventually, I'm no good to him, and he motors away. Up ahead I hear the roar of the crowd as he crosses the finish, beneath the yellow arch, arms raised overhead. He's won the stage, but what about the GC? I charge over the line 28 seconds after him. I U-turn to peer down the road. Klaus and his teammates are dots in the distance. Now it's a matter of waiting out the time gap.

We need 19 seconds more. Team Kronen thunders toward us. Ten seconds pass, then 15, then 18.

"Yeeeeeeeeeees!" I yell the entire seven seconds between Bernard's victory and Klaus's second place. The peloton glides in a half minute later.

Barely audible above the commotion of the crowd, the commentator announces, "Traveling six hundred seventy-seven miles in twenty-nine hours, thirty-four minutes, and sixteen seconds, Bernard Nagle of Image Craft–Icon has won the Tour of California!"

Tears run down my face. It's over! Bernard won, and I helped! I try to make my way to the staging area to congratulate him, but the mob makes it impossible to pass. Super Heckler Man weaves through the crowd toward me, arms waving. Oh hell, how'd he get down the mountain? The roads were closed to traffic. Wait, it's not him, but a girl dressed like him.

A special girl. Before I can dismount, she throws her arms around me and hugs me tight. I'm drenched in sweat and I must stink.

"Glory, I'm a mess."

She runs her thumb across my grainy cheek. "Sodium chloride is all, a little potassium. Are you surprised? I flew here! And I brought Daddy and your dad, too."

"My dad let you fly him here?"

"I'm a good pilot. We all wanted to see you finish."

"Awesome! What's with the . . . outfit?"

She looks down. "Oh! I thought you would think it's funny."

"More like scary. Some guy has been stalking me the

whole race." I make a show of looking on the other side of her. "Where's Alfred? I told you he could come."

"Oh, stop!" She socks my shoulder. "Poor Alfred—he's having a tough time. He turned down Harvard for the California Institute of Art, and his parents are furious. They want him to be a lawyer, and he wants to be a computer animator."

I burst out in a loud snort, and she gives me a sour look. "Sorry, babe. I'm not laughing at Alfred, honest. I'm just real happy." I get off the bike and wheel it along, holding her hand. As we inch our way toward the staging area Bernard mounts the podium and the final yellow jersey slides over his arms.

"I need to talk to you," we say simultaneously.

"You first," I tell her.

"Okay. I thought I was hurt and angry because you said I should go off to Harvard without you, when really I was mad at myself for turning it down. I never let myself believe I could get in, and now I've accepted their offer."

"Fantastic, babe! I'm so proud of you! We'll miss each other, but you'll be doing what you're meant to do. I've been thinking about my future, too." I take a deep breath. "I might want to keep racing."

She doesn't look surprised. In fact, she seems to expect it. "What would Sartre say?"

"I can."

"Uh-huh. Consequences?"

"For the longest time I've been imagining myself away at college next fall, a brand-new eighteen-year-old freshman. If I postpone that, I can never go back to that point in my life. *And* I'll be a disappointment to my parents."

"Don't be so sure of that." She nods toward the crowd ahead of us. "Your dad is damn proud of you, and who knows? Maybe your mom will come around."

I stop to look into her face. "How do you feel, Glory? What

if I never get around to college and never get farther than domestique—could you still love me?"

"I want to get back together, Evan. I just don't know what's in our future."

"Neither do I. Let's have fun finding out."

"Evan? You're going to be way better than a domestique." She takes my face in her hands and treats my dry, chapped lips to a long, luscious kiss. I'm aware of cameras snapping all around us as I wonder how a pro cyclist and a Harvard pre-med student can possibly make it together. Kristee would say it's my story. I'd say it's my life, and I love it.

". . . is Evan Boroughs," booms the announcer's voice.

We break apart and stare wide-eyed at each other. "Did you just hear my name?"

Glory nods, smiling. The realization slowly creeps into my mind as Bernard, sporting his fresh yellow jersey, shoves his way through the crowd to greet us. "Evan, what the hell are you doing? You're wanted on the podium to accept the white jersey. You're Best Young Rider!" He throws his bouquet at Glory and plants loud, sloppy kisses on both of my cheeks, just like they do in France.